For my brother Michael Henry Koch,
I love you! And I never really pushed you down the stairs!

LAST DANCE

LAST DANCE

•

Joyce & Jim Lavene

AVALON BOOKS
NEW YORK

PRINTED IN THE UNITED STATES OF AMERICA
ON ACID-FREE PAPER
BY HADDON CRAFTSMEN, BLOOMSBURG, PENNSYLVANIA

Prologue

Carrie Sommers walked out into the parking lot, glad that the prom was over. Her feet hurt in her three-inch heels, and she was tired of dragging her lacy gown around. She just wanted to crawl into some blue jeans and drive down to the beach. That's what it really meant to be a senior!

She hadn't realized that everyone else would be gone. She had stayed after the dance was over to help clean up. Her friends had been gone for an hour or longer. The parking lot was deserted, although she could hear loud music in the distance. The night was young and so were they! This was the best time of her life.

She climbed into her car and shut the door.

Chapter One

Sharyn Howard stood poised on a footstool, half of her body swathed in green satin. Three women walked around her, pinning the material and exchanging the latest gossip.

"Hold still, Sharyn!" her mother wailed for the tenth time.

"I'm not a pincushion, Mom," Sharyn returned as another pin sank into her tender flesh.

"Sheriff!" Ernie Watkins yelled, running into the room.

Sharyn's mother closed her eyes and sighed. "What do you want, Ernie?"

"S'cuse me, ma'am, but I need the sheriff to come quick. There's been a murder."

"Where?" Sharyn demanded, stepping down from

the stool to a chorus of groans and stifled complaints.

"At the school, Sheriff," Ernie told her. "It's Carrie Sommers."

Sharyn nodded, trying to wiggle out of the volumes of green satin and lace. "I'm on my way."

Sharyn Howard was the first woman to be elected sheriff in Diamond Springs, North Carolina. She followed a long history of other sheriffs who had kept the peace in the small town that had been at the foot of the Uwharrie Mountains for close to two hundred years. Two of them were her father and her grandfather. She still carried her grandfather's service revolver.

"How do you expect to have this dress ready for the reunion if you're always running off?" Aunt Selma demanded around a mouthful of stick pins.

"I'm the sheriff, Aunt Selma," Sharyn told her. "There was a murder. I have to go."

"Go on, then." Her mother waved her hand as she collapsed gracefully into a ladder-back chair. "We'll do what we can without you."

Sharyn sighed heavily. "Wait for me, Ernie."

"Yes, ma'am."

She walked back to her bedroom and closed the door, dragging out the brown and tan uniform that marked her as the sheriff. She looked at herself in the mirror on the door.

She was tall and had a square face and a body that tended to gain weight easily. The uniform had been designed for a man. She knew it did nothing for her. But it was a symbol that she had fought hard to win. She pulled it on and sat the full-brimmed brown hat on her short copper curls. Last of all, she added the holster and gun that had been passed down from her grandfather. She *was* the sheriff.

Ernie nodded respectfully, opening the door for her as her mother and aunt called out their good-byes.

"Will you be home for supper?" her mother asked.

Sharyn grimaced and took off her hat before she got into the squad car. "I'll call," she promised.

Ernie drove them down to the school. Diamond Springs High School was fifty years old and showed its age proudly with mellowed red brick and a sloping gray roof. Sharyn had graduated from the school ten years before. The school had been the site of another murder when she was a teenager. They were the only two murders in Diamond Springs that people could recall.

"What do you know about the murder?" Sharyn asked Ernie.

"Some teachers found her body this morning. They think her friends at the prom last night were the last ones to see her alive. It was bad, Sheriff."

"Bad?" Sharyn asked, knowing Ernie was always reluctant to give her any ugly details because he felt bad saying them to a woman.

"Bad," he replied, lowering his voice dramatically. "She was just a kid."

Sharyn nodded, her mouth set in a grim line. She had been the sheriff for almost two years. Diamond Springs was quiet. A few fights and a few robberies marred the lakeside town of about ten thousand people. Usually the worst crimes were fights between family members that could get violent. Sometimes even deadly.

They pulled into the school parking lot behind the medic van and the coroner's car. Another squad car was there as well. They were standing around a single bright purple sports car parked in the lot.

"Sheriff." Deputies Ed Robinson and Joe Landers greeted her with nods of their heads.

"Ed. Joe," she returned, walking up to where they stood. "How long have you been here?"

"About forty-five minutes," Ed replied. "We didn't want to leave the scene until you got here."

She nodded to the medics sitting on the edge of the van, waiting. "Where's Nick?"

Ed grinned. "In his car, I reckon. He got real tired of waiting."

She started to defend herself, then thought better of it. She was the sheriff. She got there as fast as she could. Ed and Joe had been on the job for twenty years. They knew the routine. If they had worked with her father and hadn't been eager to accept his daughter as the new sheriff that was their problem.

"Ernie," she said to the other man. "Get Nick, huh?"

Ernie nodded and ran to the coroner's car.

Sharyn could feel the deputies' eyes on her as she approached the sports car. The crime scene had been left untouched. Carrie Sommers was a beautiful girl. She was lying flat on her back on the pavement, a single flower held in her hands that rested across her chest. She was still wearing her pretty pink lace prom dress.

Her face was untouched. Her make up was still perfect, as though she had just decided to lie down on the blacktop and go to sleep. Her long blond hair was spread out around her like a halo.

"He's sleeping," Ernie told her, returning from the coroner's car.

Sharyn looked at him. "What?"

Ernie shrugged. "I called him, but he wouldn't wake up."

She heard a small laugh escape from Ed behind her, but Sharyn was unmoved. Nick Thomopolis was a good pathologist, but he was a monster to work with. He had worked with her father, and the sheriff had had nothing but praise for him. Since Sharyn had entered the scene, he had been nothing but trouble. She would have fired him, but she was worried about giving the other men the wrong impression.

Sharyn went to his car, knowing that was part of the game he was playing with her. It was something different every time. "Nick," she called out. "What is your problem?"

"Oh, Sheriff," he said, as though he was surprised that she was there. "I didn't know you were here."

"I'm here, Nick. Can we get on with it?"

"Sure, sure," he agreed readily. He climbed out of the car, the wind blowing through his coal black hair. It was streaked with fine strands of gray. "Busy getting your nails done, Sheriff?"

Sharyn ignored him as she held the door while he got his bag. "I got your resignation yesterday."

He arched one brow at her. "Good. A month is pretty short notice to find another pathologist, but I need to move on. I know you understand."

"That's fine," she replied quietly, shutting the car door behind him. "I sent the job out on the Internet. Trudy says we've already had five résumés."

"Really?" he asked, turning to look at her. "That's . . . good."

Sharyn knew him. He was surprised that she could so easily find someone else to take his place. The whole resignation was a ploy. She didn't know what he wanted from her; she thought he just enjoyed annoying her and trying to make her look stupid. Maybe she was wrong.

"Apparently, it's fashionable for pathologists to live in small towns right now," she told him.

"Next, you'll be telling me that they're all women," he quipped as they crossed the parking lot.

She stopped dead. "Look, Nick, I know you don't hate all women. I've seen you out with some. So what's the problem?"

He stopped and stared at her. "We just don't get along, Sheriff. Haven't you noticed?"

He started walking again. Sharyn had no choice but to hurry after him. Whatever his problem was, she was going to be glad to see the back of him!

The wind blew off Diamond Mountain Lake. The lake acted as a backdrop for the school and grounds. It was surrounded on three sides by mist-shrouded mountains. The open side had a beach and picnic area that ran almost to the school grounds, then was lost in forest and rocks.

The air smelled like rain with a touch of late spring cold that could mean frost on the peach trees too late in the year. A few stray white blossoms blew down from the plum trees that surrounded the parking lot. Sharyn watched them dance across the pavement and the hood of the purple sports car.

Nick knelt beside the body and pulled on his latex gloves. "What do you think, Sheriff?"

It was a game they played. A test, of sorts, to decide if she was competent to be the sheriff. At least that was the way she'd come to see it. Nick was constantly trying to outthink her, outguess her, and generally, outwit her. She knew the other men always listened and even laid bets from time to time on the outcome. Fortunately she caught on quickly and gave as good as she got.

Sharyn knelt down beside him, careful of the area around the body. "I'd bet that she was killed here, then laid out next to the car as some sort of atonement for the act. She still has her pocketbook." She picked up the tiny beaded holder and opened it. "Car keys. Lipstick. A mirror. Driver's license and fifty dollars in cash." She put the contents into a plastic evidence bag that Ernie held for her, then put the purse into a separate bag. "We'll have to check with her friends to see if anything is missing."

A photographic flash went off behind her as Joe took pictures of the crime scene. It was like a memory breaking through in her brain as she thought about the last murder that had happened in that parking lot.

"Sheriff?" Nick chided, bringing her back to the present.

"Sorry, I was thinking about something else."

"Sure," he answered softly. "No problem. I always drift off while I'm kneeling down next to a dead body."

She frowned at him. "I was thinking how much this reminds me of another murder that happened right here ten years ago."

"Leila Bentley," Joe supplied.

"Exactly," she agreed. "She was killed and laid out just like this."

"Not just like this," Ed corrected. "I was there with your daddy. It was different."

"Maybe," she admitted. "But it was very similar." She looked at Carrie Sommers' dead face. "She even looks like Leila."

"That one's over, Sheriff," Joe told her plainly. "That old boy's getting ready to find his way out of this world in a few days for what he did to that little girl. This is different."

Sharyn shook her head. "Well, that may be, but the similarity is striking."

Nick sighed. "What else, Sheriff? Or is that your way of saying you don't see anything else here?"

"The killer was meticulous," she said, concentrating on the scene around her. "No blood or dirt on her face or in her hair." She picked up the girl's hands and looked under the nails. They were clean and powder pink. "She didn't have time to fight."

"Around the neck." Nick indicated with his hand. "Ligature marks. It looks as though she was strangled. Yet there's no sign of a struggle." He moved carefully to lift the girl's head. "Probably head trauma. Hit from behind. Unconscious before she was strangled."

"He or she was very careful," Sharyn agreed. "Check her for sexual assault."

"I can tell you now that she wasn't," Nick replied lazily as Sharyn got to her feet.

"How's that?"

"Look at her dress. Pulled down nice and spread out around her. She wasn't assaulted."

Sharyn followed his gaze down to the girl's pink heels still on her feet. "How long do you think she's been dead?"

Nick moved the girl's head back down, then examined her briefly. "I'd say we're talking between midnight and two A.M. for time of death."

"Prom was over at about twelve-thirty," Joe added. "There were still people hanging around at one A.M. when David made his patrol through here last night. I called him and checked before I left the station."

"Could he mark if this car was here then?" Sharyn asked.

Joe shook his head. "Nope. Said there were still quite a few cars up here then. He had a call about the noise around that time. Otherwise, it was quiet last night."

"Too quiet." Sharyn considered, looking at the girl's body.

"She's still wearing a good watch and an expensive ring." Nick called their attention back. "It obviously wasn't robbery."

"What idiot would hold someone up, kill her,

then lay her out with a flower in her hand?" Ed demanded.

Sharyn looked around the area. "See if you can find out where the flower came from. I don't know a lot about flowers, but it doesn't look wild to me."

"Shouldn't she have been wearing a corsage?" Joe asked.

"Maybe that's it," Sharyn agreed. It was a small pink and white flower that could have been part of a corsage. "Check around and see if there's any more of it."

"Can we transport so I can get started?" Nick asked.

"That's fine," she replied. "Ed and Joe will go over the scene. Send the tow truck for the car and we'll go over it in impound." She started to walk away.

"Heading back to the salon, Sheriff?" Nick asked caustically.

She turned back to him. "I'm going to tell this girl's parents that their baby is dead. Want to come?"

Nick looked away, then signaled the medic to get the body.

There were times that Sharyn might have bantered acidic remarks with the man, or even made a wager on something Nick theorized. This wasn't one of them. Looking at the girl's face was too sad. It was such a waste. She shivered in the cold wind.

She felt Ed and Joe staring after her. She knew Nick was smirking. She didn't care. Seeing that girl lying there reminded her too much of Leila Bentley. It had been a long time, but she hadn't forgotten. And she wasn't made of stone.

Ernie loped up beside Sharyn's long stride through the parking lot and climbed behind the wheel of the cruiser to take her to Carrie's house. He was a short, wiry man with hardly a sprig of hair on his head and a large pointed nose. He'd worked with Sharyn's father as well. But from the day Sharyn had stepped into the office, Ernie had been there for her. He could turn paperwork around faster than anyone else she knew, and he kept his ear to the ground. If there was something to know about a case, Ernie knew it.

"What do you know about Carrie Sommers and her family?" Sharyn asked, thinking about what she knew of them. She knew Carrie's father was a car salesman. He and his brother owned the huge Ford dealership in town. Carrie probably always drove a new car.

"She was a good student," Ernie replied. "Had a good scholarship lined up for college. Dated the same boy for the past two years, Tim Stryker. She was a cheerleader and the homecoming queen. I think she tried out for Miss North Carolina. Never in any trouble."

Sharyn shivered again. Like Leila.

"Catching something, Sheriff?" Ernie wondered, seeing the chill.

"I don't know," she admitted. He was the only man on the job that she would have admitted it to. "It just reminds me so much of Leila Bentley."

"You went to school with her, didn't you?" he asked.

Sharyn nodded. "We were the same age. I remember Dad investigating her murder."

"It was a terrible time for everyone. The whole town was different then. Closer, I guess. No one could believe that something like that could happen here."

"That's why everyone was so relieved that the guy who did it wasn't from here."

He nodded. "It set everyone's mind at ease."

"Maybe they were too quick to want to be at ease," she answered thoughtfully.

"What are you saying, Sheriff?"

"I don't know yet," Sharyn told him as they pulled into the Sommers' drive. "I just don't know."

Telling anyone they had lost a loved one wasn't easy. Sometimes it was her job to tell the family about a loved one who had drowned in the lake. Sometimes it was a car accident on the highway. The saddest was telling parents about the loss of a child. In this case, there couldn't have been anything worse. The Sommers' beautiful, intelligent daughter with a bright future had been murdered, alone and helpless in parking lot where she should have been safe.

"Yes?" Cara Sommers asked as she opened the heavy door with its beautiful stained glass windowpanes.

"Mrs. Sommers," Sharyn began.

"Sheriff? Is there a problem? I know the kids went down to Myrtle. Has there been a problem?"

Sharyn looked down at her hands, then back up at the other woman's face. "I don't know how to tell you this, Mrs. Sommers. Carrie was found in the school parking lot this morning. She was murdered."

"Oh Sheriff, there must be some mistake," Cara argued, her smile fading like the sunrise. "Carrie left last night with her friends to go to the beach. She's down there now. We can call her."

"Mrs. Sommers."

"Let me call Charlie. He'll know what to do."

"We can come in, if you like, and talk to him," Sharyn volunteered. "I can answer any questions that I know about right now."

"Please," Cara invited them. "You'll want to hear what Charlie has to say. He knows that Carrie is at the beach."

"Sheriff. Deputy." Charlie Sommers approached them as they started into the foyer. "What seems to be the problem?"

Sharyn looked squarely at the man. "Mr. Sommers, I'm sorry to tell you that your daughter is dead. We found her body in the parking lot at the school this morning."

Charlie Sommers looked at his wife. "That can't be. She's at the beach."

Ernie stepped forward with a picture of the crime scene. Cara Sommers collapsed in her husband's arms, sobbing hysterically.

"I'm sorry, Mr. Sommers." Sharyn addressed the man. "But we do need to talk to you as soon as possible."

Charlie Sommers' face was deathly white as he held his hysterical wife to him. "Let me get her settled and call the doctor. I'll come back down."

Sharyn and Ernie waited in the foyer, not speaking. The face of death was always familiar, but it became vividly real when it came to addressing the needs of the family. To everyone else, Carrie Sommers had become a murder to be solved. To her parents, she was a hope for life, lost forever.

Half an hour later, outwardly composed but showing signs of strain, Charlie Sommers returned and led them into the formal living room. "I don't know what to say."

Sharyn sat forward in her chair. "You have our sincere sympathy, Mr. Sommers. And I wouldn't bother you or your wife at this time, but the sooner we get the information we need, the sooner we can catch the person who did this thing to your daughter."

"I know," he agreed. "I just don't. . . ." He swallowed hard and faced them, his eyes flooded with tears. "What do I do now, Sheriff?"

Sharyn crouched down before him and took his hands in hers. "Help us first, Mr. Sommers. Then we'll help you attend to your daughter. The coroner has her right now. Her body won't be released until he's done. This is the only thing you can do for Carrie right now."

He nodded wordlessly and struggled to gain some composure. "H-how did she die?"

"We think she was strangled, sir," Sharyn told him gently. "We'll know more after the autopsy."

"Of course, of course," he repeated in agony. "She got accepted to Duke last week. Proudest day of my life."

Sharyn swallowed hard. "I need to ask you some questions, sir. Give me the best answers you can," she counseled. "We'll go from there."

"All right," he managed to say. "What can I tell you?"

Ernie took notes while they determined what time he had seen his daughter last. He had been at the office when she had gone to the prom, but he knew her mother had been there and had taken pictures of Carrie and her date, Tim Stryker, before they had left for the prom.

"You don't think it could have been him, do you?" he asked plaintively.

Sharyn squeezed his hand. "We'll check out all the possibilities. Is there any reason you would ask that? Was there a history of violence between them?"

"No," he denied. "Not as far as I know. He always seemed the perfect gentleman when I saw him. Of course, Cara would know better." His face twisted. "If I thought that it was him—"

"You'll have to let us do our job, Mr. Sommers. Don't do anything that might jeopardize our finding Carrie's killer and bringing him to justice. Your wife shouldn't be alone at a time like this."

"I won't." He shuddered and folded his arms across his chest.

"Do you know what the plan was for after the prom? Who was she meeting, and where was she supposed to meet them?" Sharyn tried to divert him.

"I'm not sure," he admitted, struggling to stay calm. "My wife would know. She keeps track of things like that. Maybe later—"

"We'll come back after she's had a chance to absorb some of the shock. What kind of car did your daughter drive?"

It was the same car that they had found parked in the lot next to her body. There didn't seem to be any surprises. The girl was supposed to go to the prom, then meet her friends on the way to Myrtle

Beach. Just like a thousand or so other kids on prom night. It just hadn't worked out the way she had planned.

Sharyn nodded to Ernie, and he closed his notebook. "We'll probably have more questions as we go along, Mr. Sommers. If you could get us some information about where Carrie was supposed to be staying at the beach, her friends' names and addresses and anything else that may give us a start looking into this for you."

"I'll do what I can, Sheriff," he replied. "I can offer a reward if that will help. I want to get whoever did this to Carrie."

Sharyn shook her head. "We'll talk about that later. Let's see how it goes. Okay?"

"Thanks." He shook her hand. "You'll let us know . . . about Carrie, I mean."

"We will," she promised.

They let themselves out into the increasingly cloudy day. The wind had picked up, and the cold had deepened.

"How could something like this happen to a kid like that?" Ernie muttered, thrusting his notebook into the car with an angry push.

Sharyn got into the car. "I don't know," she answered. "Let's go back over to the school."

"They probably got most of everything hauled away by now," Ernie told her, wondering what she was looking for.

"That's true, but let's take a look at what's left."

They pulled into the parking lot. Carrie's body was gone. The other squad car, as well as Nick's car and the medics', were gone. A spray cleaning service was just pulling up to clean the parking lot. Sharyn sent Ernie to stop them until she was done looking around.

Carrie's car was still parked in the same place. A chalk outline marked the place where her body had been on the pavement.

Why had the girl been walking on the passenger side of the car? Sharyn wondered.

If she'd been alone and about to drive down and meet her friends, she would have been walking to the driver's side.

She opened the car door. It was unlocked. There was a profusion of school books and empty soda bottles, make up and a sweater and jeans in the back seat. The interior was clean, though. Not a mark on it. The car would be towed in and inspected minutely, but it looked as though nothing had happened inside.

Sharyn sat behind the wheel and looked through the windshield. Carrie had parked close to the school. She must have been there early. She might have been on the prom committee, which could account for her being there late as well. They would have to check that out.

There didn't seem to be any sign of a struggle to

get the girl out of the car. Sharyn walked around the exterior and checked the paint and the chrome. The body had been less than a foot away from the side of the car, yet there were no visible signs of trauma. It was possible they might find hair or tissue samples with a closer look.

The hood wasn't latched down. That seemed a little peculiar but might not mean anything. She didn't touch it but left instructions to check it for prints or fiber remnants. The killer might have strangled the girl against the hood and caused it to pop open.

The car keys had been in her purse. Whoever killed her hadn't wanted her car. They'd left fifty dollars cash and driver's license behind. They hadn't killed her for money. If Nick was right, and he usually was about those things, Carrie hadn't been raped. That left only a personal motive for her death. Sharyn didn't even want to think of a personal motive for murdering an eighteen-year-old girl.

"Finished?" Ernie asked as she came walking back to the car.

She nodded. "I don't want the lot cleaned until the car is gone, though. Get on the line and see what's keeping the garage from picking it up. I'll talk to the sweepers."

The men in the sweeper truck didn't like having their timetable messed up, but Sharyn was the sheriff and they didn't have much choice. They huffed a lot, but in the end, they moved the truck to the next site.

"The garage has somebody on the way out for the car," Ernie told her. "What next?"

Sharyn glanced at her watch. "Let's head over to the hospital and see what Nick's found."

Chapter Two

Nick was hunched over a cup of coffee and a plastic bag of jewelry when Sharyn stepped into his office. He hadn't answered when she had knocked at the door. He didn't look up when she called his name. He was still wearing his protective plastic goggles.

"Nick?" she called, wondering if this was a new game or if he was as deep in thought as he appeared to be. "Nick, I'd hate to have to slap you to get your attention."

He looked up at that and shrugged as though he really were surprised to see her there. "Sorry. Lost in thought, I guess."

"Carrie Sommers?" She motioned to the jewelry in the plastic bag.

"Yeah," he answered briefly, ripping the glasses

from his face. "One ring. One watch. A few bobby pins. And two fake nails. I guess she wasn't perfect after all, huh?"

Sharyn slammed his office door. "Will you stop? Doesn't anything get to you?"

Nick stood up and pushed his chair back hard. The legs scraped on the old tile floor. "Not everyone shows their trauma by getting a manicure or having their hair done, Sheriff," he growled at her. "Some of us get by the best we can."

They stared at one another. Sharyn looked away. "What did you find?"

Nick picked up the report that was on the top of his cluttered desk. "It's all in there. She wasn't violated. There was blunt force trauma to the back of the head. It probably knocked her unconscious. She was strangled using a great deal of force. There were fibers embedded into her throat. I think from these." He tossed another plastic bag on top of the report.

"Are you telling me she was strangled with her own pantyhose, then the killer put them back on her but never touched her sexually?"

He nodded. "That's what I'm telling you. All laid out nice and neat when he was done."

"He?" she wondered with a lift of her cinnamon-colored eyebrow.

"He," Nick conjectured. "There was a lot of

power involved with the strangulation. This is a strong man. A great deal of forearm strength."

Sharyn glanced around the tiny office. "So, he must have hit her with whatever it was in the back of the head and started to move her before he realized that he wasn't wearing gloves?"

"Something like that. And I think I can even help with the kind of gloves. Not rubber or latex. There were some gray cotton fibers on her dress and hands. I think he wore some kind of work glove. Maybe a gardening glove."

Something was pushing at the envelope of her memory. "Nick," she began, facing him with desperation in her hazel eyes.

"What?" he asked, as though it mattered that something was wrong.

"I know you and I have had our differences but I want to ask you to do me a favor."

He looked down at the desktop. "I'm at your beck and call, Sheriff."

She grimaced. "I guess for now, at least, that's true. But this is something—well, nobody else is going to like it very much. I don't like it at all."

He was genuinely confused and interested. "What is it?"

"There's a case. It's ten years old."

"The case you were talking about this morning," he recalled with a smug look on his dark face.

"Leila Bentley. It might just be a figment of my

imagination, but it seems to me that this case is too similar to be a fluke."

"You want me to look over the autopsy results," he guessed.

"And keep your mouth shut," she added.

He looked at her. They were roughly the same height. Her copper red curls gleamed in the dingy overhead lighting. The freckles on her face didn't belie her sincerity. He sighed. "What's the name?"

"Leila Bentley. It happened ten years ago. She was found in the school parking lot the same way we found Carrie this morning."

He wrote down the name and date, then looked back at her. "And you went to school with this Bentley girl?"

"We weren't friends, but I knew her. It's a small school."

"That would have been a big conviction for your father," he remarked.

"Don't remind me." She frowned. "That's one reason I need this kept quiet for now. If I'm wrong—"

"You buy me dinner for my trouble," he interjected. "And no one knows the difference."

"But if I'm right..." She sighed and turned away.

"Life gets much more complicated?" he suggested.

"Yeah," she agreed with a faint smile. "Thanks, Nick."

"Yeah, I'm too good for you, Sheriff," he mocked.

"Is that why you're leaving?" she wondered seriously.

"Something like that," he told her, not giving anything away.

Sharyn didn't try any harder to understand him. He was good at what he did. She hated to lose him. Although she wouldn't be the one to tell him that. She slipped out the side door, avoiding the front of the building. A crowd of reporters from the local television station and the newspaper were already looking for answers. Great! She slapped her hand on the car door before she opened it. With the media all over it, the case would be even harder to work.

Ernie skirted the edge of the parking lot and took a side road to the main road that ran through town. A cold rain had begun to fall as twilight settled across the rolling Uwharries.

"This could freeze tonight," he said as the moments passed and Sharyn kept silent.

"Yeah," she agreed. She wasn't sure if she should tell anyone else, even Ernie, that she was seriously thinking about opening Leila Bentley's case again. It would hinge largely on whatever Nick could tell her. In the meantime, she had a present-day murder to solve.

"We got the report from impound," Ernie said, wondering if she and Nick had been arguing again. It would be just as well for everyone if Nick Thomopolis did leave Diamond Springs. He'd been a thorn in the sheriff's side since she took office.

"Anything?" she wondered.

"Apparently, there was no impact that they could find anywhere on the car. They looked over the hood area thoroughly, but all they could find were some gray cotton threads that didn't seem to match anything else in or on the car."

Sharyn nodded. "Nick found some gray cotton threads on the girl's body. He thinks it might be from work gloves. Maybe garden gloves."

Ernie shrugged. "The kind they sell for a dollar at the discount store that everyone has at one time or another."

"That's about it," she agreed with a yawn. She told him the rest of the findings that Nick had given her. But she kept her own peace on asking the coroner to look into Leila's murder. Hopefully, Nick would respect her wishes on keeping that quiet as well.

They got back to the sheriff's office at about seven P.M. The light rain had turned to freezing mush on the roads. But the reporters were still out in force.

"How can there be so many of them here when

there were so many of them at the hospital?" Ernie asked her.

"I think they always make two of them at a time," she quipped with a small smile. "Let's see what's come in and what Ed and Joe found, then we'll issue a statement."

They squeezed past the reporters at the door, Ernie turning back to promise them a statement later that night. Trudy handed Sharyn her calls, which included several from her mother and one from Charlie Sommers.

"That Stryker kid is here," Ed told her. "He's been waiting to see you. Something about Carrie's dad asking him if he murdered her."

"Great," Sharyn replied, taking her messages and shaking her head when Trudy asked if she wanted a cup of coffee.

"You haven't eaten since I picked you up," Ernie reminded her briefly.

She grimaced. "They're making my class reunion dress a size smaller than I wear, Ernie. I can't eat again until after the eighteenth."

Ernie smiled and shook his head as he followed her into her office where Joe was already waiting for her. He shut the door when they were all inside. This was going to be a big case with the media. It wouldn't help for little fragments of information to sneak out of the office.

"So." Sharyn took a deep breath as she sat down

at her father's massive oak desk. "What do we have so far?"

Ed gave her the rundown on the flowers that Carrie had been holding. It had been part of a corsage. The rest of it seemed to be in the dumpster. He had sent it out to be analyzed for fingerprints or fiber samples. The dumpster was clean. Not even the lint that they had found on the car and the body was present on the garbage container.

Joe had spoken with the teachers who had found Carrie's body that morning. They had been coming in for a special event that was canceled with the discovery. Neither one of the teachers had been present at the prom the night before. Neither one of them was Carrie's teacher, so the information they could provide was limited.

"Okay," Sharyn said when they had finished their preliminary reports. "I'm going to issue a statement on this. Basically that the girl was found dead, and that we're looking into it with no suspects at the time. I don't want this part about her not being sexually assaulted leaking to the press. It could be something that we can use in the investigation. Everyone's going to assume that she was assaulted since she was so young and pretty. Any questions?"

Joe nodded his head. He was in his late forties and kept his dark hair cut to military length. He had a strong jaw and a powerful sense of right and wrong. "I got a list of the girl's friends. The people

I talked to didn't think she had any enemies. Apparently, she was well liked."

"We need to start lining them up for interviews. I'd like to know who was with her at the dance, and what all of them were wearing. Especially the ones who helped with the clean-up activities afterwards. Someone might have seen something and doesn't realize it."

"I have interviews set up with each of her teachers and the school principal, as well as her faculty advisor and her minister," Ed Robinson told her briefly. "She was involved in a lot of clubs and stuff. I'm seeing all of them in the next couple of days."

She nodded. "That sounds good." She looked up at him. Ed was well liked in the department. He was tall, thin, and had a head full of curly blond hair that he kept to a manageable length. More than one woman had been left sighing over his baby blue eyes and dimpled smile. He had worked with her father as well, but he was younger than Joe was. Not that she had managed to establish more than a working rapport with him.

"Check out the adults who were involved with the prom as well. You know there were a handful of advisors and chaperones. Someone was there with the kids while they were cleaning up after the prom. They should have left after Carrie did, and they might not have realized what happened."

"I'm out of here," Joe said standing and stretching his long limbs. "See you tomorrow."

Ed nodded and left after the other man. "Sheriff."

"Thanks, Ed, Joe," she added as they walked out of the office door. She sighed. At least they worked well together. She looked up at the pictures of previous sheriffs on the wall. Her father, T. Raymond Howard smiled down at her. "It was easy for you, wasn't it?"

Her grandfather, Jacob Howard, scowled and held up his gun for the picture on the wall. He was the first sheriff actually elected in Diamond Springs; the rest had been appointed. When she was a little girl, he had told her that he'd looked like that in the picture to scare people into telling him what he needed to know.

"Sheriff?" Ernie put his head around the door. "I called the Sommerses. Mr. Sommers thinks you can come out and talk with his wife tomorrow."

Sharyn stood up from her chair. "We'll see what else comes up after I talk to Tim Stryker. I'd rather not bother them again. They're going through enough without us questioning them every five minutes."

"Okay, I'm heading for home," Ernie told her with a smile. "Can I get you anything before I go?"

"No, I'm fine," she answered with a return smile. What would she do without Ernie?

"Are you going to talk to the Stryker boy before you leave?" he wondered.

"Yeah, but I'll be fine alone, Ernie. I don't think Tim Stryker is a murderer."

Deputy David Matthews came in for the evening. He was checking his messages when Sharyn came out of her office. "Sheriff." He nodded, glancing up at her.

"David," she acknowledged.

"That's a crowd at the door," he told her.

"Yeah. Did Ed fill you in?"

David shook his head. He was a stocky man with thick brown hair and a thick brown moustache. He graduated from high school the same year as Sharyn and being the new man on the team, he always got the graveyard shift. Not that there was much to do. Usually, Diamond Springs was quiet at night. "It's some terrible business, Sheriff."

"I've got the girl's boyfriend in the interrogation room now," she added. "Would you like to sit in with me while I talk to him?"

He glanced around the quiet office. Only the emergency dispatcher was left for the night. "I was on my way out on patrol, Sheriff. Ed said I should keep my eye out around the lake."

"That's fine," she said with a forced smile.

"You think this boy could have something to do with it?" he wondered.

"I really don't," she admitted. "But I need to talk

to him. He might have been the last one to see her alive."

"I could stay," he volunteered.

"No, you're right," she told him. "Go ahead and take care of your regular patrol. I don't know what Ed has in mind about the lake, but with these reporters in town stirring things up, we better keep an extra eye out."

"I'll be going then, Sheriff," he told her.

"Okay, good night."

She watched him walk back out of the office and wished that she could find some way to reach him. Despite their ages being so close and having experiences in common in high school, they were the most distant in the office. David had been with the office only a year longer, but he resented her a decade more.

"Sheriff?" Trudy called as she was about to walk out the door. "Your mother called again. She's holding dinner for you."

"Thanks, Trudy," Sharyn replied, shaking herself out of her depressing job evaluation. "I'll see you tomorrow."

Sharyn picked up the phone and called her mother, quickly telling her not to wait for supper. She wasn't sure what time she was going to be home, but it wouldn't be for a while.

"I planned on you having another fitting for your dress tomorrow," Faye Howard told her eldest, most difficult daughter.

"There won't be time for that tomorrow," Sharyn told her mother bluntly. "A girl is dead, Mom. I'll have to be on this case for the next few days, without dress fittings."

Her mother made it clear what she thought about Sharyn's attitude, then hung up, saying she was going to eat her cold supper.

Sharyn rubbed her tired eyes and pushed the conversation to the back of her mind. With the press on this thing, there was going to be pressure to solve this murder as quickly as possible. Not that she didn't want to have the culprit locked up and off the streets. But sometimes people wanted miracles, and those were hard to find.

She opened the door to the interrogation room, and the boy who had been sitting inside jumped up. "Tim?"

"Yes," he answered. "Tim Stryker, Sheriff. I am—I was—Carrie's boyfriend."

"Sit down," she invited, taking a seat herself. The wooden table they sat at was scarred with years of use. The chairs were uncomfortable. She wished that she could have talked to the boy in his own house. There was no reason for him to be so jumpy.

"I heard about Carrie when I came back from Myrtle this afternoon. The first thing I did was go over to her house. Her father threatened to kill me if I was the one who hurt Carrie. But I didn't hurt her, Sheriff. I loved Carrie. We were going to be married someday."

"I believe you," Sharyn told him quietly. She wasn't going to get any decent answers from him if he didn't calm down. "I would like to ask you a few questions since you're here. I know you want to help us find who did this to Carrie."

"I'd kill him," he told her painfully. "How could anyone hurt Carrie?"

He broke down sobbing, and Sharyn excused herself and went to the break room to get him a soda. He had stopped crying when she returned. He took a few sips of the drink.

"Now," she started again. "Just calm down. Take a deep breath. I know this is terrible for you, but we have to stay focused on finding Carrie's killer."

"Okay," he agreed miserably, taking another swig of soda. "Just ask me what you need to know."

"When was the last time you saw Carrie?" she wondered, pulling out her notebook.

"Just before the end of the dance. She was staying for the cleanup. She helped out on the decorations committee. I left before her because I was going to a party before I met her on the way to the beach. A bunch of us were meeting to drive down together."

"Can you give me the names of the people who helped out on the decorations committee?" she asked.

He took another stiff gulp of soda. "Sure, I can write them all down."

"Good." She handed him a yellow legal pad. "Write down those names and the names of the chaperones. Then write down everyone's name who you can recall was still at the dance when you left. People in the parking lot, people in the school."

Sharyn waited, watching him while he wrote. He wasn't the captain of the football team, obviously. He was a thin boy with wild hair and intelligent eyes. He was dressed well. Expensively. She didn't know anything about his family, but he seemed to be a good kid.

"So, you planned to meet Carrie on the way to the beach?" she asked when he had finished.

He shook his head. "There were so many parties last night. A bunch of us were going to the beach together in Sam's van. But we were all driving to the Point and parking in the boat lot there. It's not too busy this time of year."

"Why didn't you wait for Carrie?"

He swallowed hard on another bout of tears. "When she didn't show up, I figured she was at a party and wasn't going down with us. There were a few people who didn't show up at the Point. We talked about just going on if someone wasn't there to go in the van. Everybody had their own cars."

"Can you make me a list of the others who didn't show up at the Point?"

"Sure," he agreed. "We all got down to the beach, and I realized that Carrie didn't make it. I called a few of her friends who didn't want to go to the beach or couldn't go. They hadn't seen her. I thought she could have had car trouble. So I came back home looking for her."

"Write down the names of those kids who couldn't go as well," she instructed while he was writing.

"I couldn't believe when Mr. Sommers accused me of killing Carrie," he told her again. "Why would he think that?"

"Because he's hurt and he wants to find who did this to her," Sharyn explained briefly. "Just like what you told me before about killing whoever did this. He feels the same."

He nodded and swallowed more soda. "I kissed her good-bye at the dance. She looked so beautiful." He looked up at Sharyn. "I loved her so much."

"I know you did," Sharyn sympathized. "But I want you to go home and get some sleep. It's going to be a very emotional time for everyone in the next few days. And I don't want to hear you say something stupid again like you're going to kill anyone. I'm sure Carrie wouldn't want you to ruin your life for her."

He looked at her with drowned blue eyes. "I know."

"If you think of anything, anything that might be

useful or seemed out of the ordinary, call me," she told him, pressing her card into his hand. "Don't worry about it sounding silly. If you hear anything from another one of Carrie's friends that they don't want to tell me, I want you to tell me. Maybe we can find who really did this to her and lock them up."

"I'll stay on top of it," he told her firmly. "Can I take the rest of the soda?"

"Sure thing, Tim. Thanks for coming in."

She watched him leave the office, then yawned and gathered her things together to leave. It had been a long day. A few of the die-hard reporters had stayed the night on the front lawn of the sheriff's office. Most had gone home. The few that had stayed were surprised when she knocked at the van window.

"I have a statement to make," she advised them.

There was a flurry of activity as they ran to set up cameras and nudge sleeping editors. Finally, when they were ready, Sharyn put on her hat and issued her statement.

"At about ten A.M. this morning, the body of Carolyn Sommers, age eighteen, was found in the high school parking lot next to her car. She had been murdered by person or persons unknown. The sheriff's department is investigating."

"How was she killed, Sheriff?"

"She was strangled," Sharyn explained.

"Do you think there could be someone out there looking for young women to strangle, or was this personal?"

"I don't think anyone should panic over this. It appears to be an isolated case."

An isolated case. Sharyn considered her words as she drove home in a squad car. She didn't really believe that was true, but she wasn't going public with her real feelings about the case. No one else knew besides Nick. She only hoped she hadn't made a mistake in trusting him with the knowledge. It could be a good opportunity to make her look foolish.

Without thinking about it, she drove back to the school. There was a sliver of a moon coming up across the mountains, shadowing the lake and the trees that rose up immediately behind the old building. She parked in the lot and turned off her headlights, thinking about the past.

Leila Bentley had been killed ten years ago on the night of the senior prom. Her body had been found in the parking lot the next morning. Her corsage had been entwined in her hair. Her arms had been folded over her chest. Everyone said that she had looked as though she had fallen asleep on the cold, hard ground.

Sharyn had been at the prom that night. But not in Leila's circle of friends that included the cheerleaders and the other cool kids in their graduating class.

Not even being the sheriff's daughter could make her cool. She'd been slightly overweight, full of pimples and a bad attitude. Her mother had insisted on her wearing her hair too long, and the heavy curls didn't help the matter.

Still, when the strap had broken on Sharyn's terrible black gown that night, Leila had been the one in the powder room who had helped her. Sharyn could remember her pretty face and sweet smile as she had found a pin for the strap. It was impossible not to like Leila, despite all of her accomplishments and her beauty. She was just a nice person. Not at all like the image of the popular beauty queen that Sharyn had considered her to be.

Sharyn hadn't been there when they had found Leila's body. Most of the information she had, she had gotten from the papers and the gossip at school. Her father had always refused to talk about his cases at home. He had been especially tight-lipped about Leila's murder.

But when she had seen Carrie's pretty face that morning, everything seemed to come together. True, it had been ten years since Leila's murder. True, Leila's killer was up in Raleigh waiting for his own death by electrocution. To say that Ronnie Smith hadn't been Leila's killer was to say that her father had been wrong.

And if those things weren't true, they had been harboring a killer in Diamond Springs for the past ten years.

Chapter Three

At seven A.M. the next morning, Sharyn was up and on the phone with George Albert, the city councilman who represented Diamond Springs. He had been a friend of the family for as long as Sharyn could remember. She had valued his advice since her father died. It was George who had encouraged her to run for the sheriff's office.

"What a terrible thing," George said sympathetically. "Especially for this to happen here."

"I know," Sharyn agreed. "It was terrible telling Carrie's parents yesterday. Her mother was hysterical."

"I spoke with Charlie last night. I think she's calmed down a lot. They're getting everything together for her funeral. What a waste! She was such a pretty, bright young thing."

"It's not the first time it's happened," Sharyn told him quietly.

"What are you saying?" he asked her.

"I'm talking about Leila Bentley's murder ten years ago. She was found in the same parking lot. I think the murder pattern might have been the same."

George took a moment to digest her words. "Are you telling me that you think the same person was responsible for both murders?"

"I don't know," she admitted, pulling her robe closer around herself. She was sitting at the kitchen table, reading the bold headlines about Carrie's murder in the paper and drinking coffee.

"Wasn't the man caught and sentenced to die who did that other murder, Sharyn?" he asked.

"There was a man who was convicted of the crime," she agreed. "He is scheduled to die later this month, I think. But the cases are so close, George. What if they were wrong?"

"You mean what if your father was wrong?" He added depth to the words.

"All right," she said. "What if my father was wrong? What if they had the wrong man?"

George whistled slowly. "I think you better have a world of proof before you stir up that hornet's nest, young lady. There are a few people here who wouldn't want to relive that case and wouldn't want to have that conviction questioned."

"I know that," she replied slowly. "And maybe

I'm wrong. It's just a feeling that I have, George. I can't ignore it."

"You've got good instincts, Sharyn," he commended. "Use them. Your father would want you to do that."

"Even if it meant overturning his biggest case?"

"Especially if it meant finding a killer and setting an innocent man free. Your father did the best he could. He surely wasn't perfect, and he would have been the first person to tell you that. But be careful. You could make some enemies with this. Check your facts and double-check them before you release any word of this."

"You know I will."

"Then do the best you can," he advised her. "I have some news."

"Something good, I hope," Sharyn encouraged.

"Richard's home."

Sharyn tried to suppress her surprise. Richard was Brenda and George's only son. He was born prematurely, and was sickly and small for most of his childhood. Sharyn had always stood a head taller than him. Unfortunately, they'd sent him away when they couldn't control him anymore. Since their parents were close, she'd spent time with him as a child. He'd been a strange, quiet child.

"That's good," she mustered for his benefit.

"He's different now, Sharyn. It's the new drugs. He's a whole other person. It's a miracle."

Sharyn had once seen the boy kill a mouse with a sharp stick. It had been *her* mouse. She was reserving judgment. "I'm glad for you, George. And I know Brenda's happy."

"You'll have to come over for dinner, Sharyn. You'll be able to see for yourself."

"I'll do that, George. Probably when this case is over."

He agreed. "Good luck, Sheriff."

Sharyn put down the phone and folded the newspaper closed. How long had it been since they sent Richard away?

She glanced up. Faye Howard was standing across from her, glaring at her.

"What are you doing, Sharyn?" she demanded. Her pink dress was pressed and fresh. Her make up was perfect, and her hair had been carefully arranged in neat brown curls on her head.

"Finishing my coffee," her daughter responded lazily. "It's Sunday. I have to go into the office, but I'm not going in before eight."

"You know what I mean," her mother told her angrily. "How dare you dishonor your father's memory?"

Sharyn rubbed her hand across her eyes. "I haven't dishonored anything, Mom. But it's possible one of Dad's arrests was wrong."

"Are you talking about that poor girl's murder?"

"Yes," Sharyn responded. "Leila Bentley."

"I know you went to *college*, Sharyn," her mother accused as though college were a dirty word. "And I know you think you know it all, but your father's record stands on its own. He was the sheriff here for almost thirty years. He didn't make mistakes."

"Of course he did, Mom," Sharyn said defensively. "He was just human. There was a lot of pressure on him to make an arrest in that case. He may have been influenced by it."

"How can you sit in this house, *his* house, and say those things?" her mother demanded. "It is beyond my comprehension."

Sharyn sighed. She hadn't meant her mother to hear about this until later. She didn't want a world war started between them because of a feeling she had about Carrie Sommers' murder.

"I don't know for sure yet, Mom." She tried to pacify her indignant parent. "I'm just working through this Sommers case."

"Leave the other case out of it, Sharyn," her mother commanded. "Please. For the sake of your father's memory."

Sharyn looked at her and wanted to oblige. "I can't, Mom," she said carefully. "If I find out they don't mesh, I won't pursue it. If they do, I won't have any choice."

Her mother gave her a withering look, then stormed from the room, slamming the door behind her.

Sharyn finished her coffee, skipped the low-fat bran muffin she had planned to eat and went to her room to get dressed.

The pink granite courthouse shone in the sun. Beside it, the smaller sheriff's office was made of the same material. A spreading magnolia dominated the grounds. Picnic tables, not much in use during the winter, dotted the brown grass. The wind was just as cold as it had been the day before, heavy with the promise of more frozen precipitation. But the media stood outside the door waiting to ask questions.

Sharyn had talked to Ernie before she'd left for the office. She knew about the crowd and avoided it by parking in the impound lot behind the station and walking in the back door. No one could get into the lot without authorization. It might have to be her safe haven until the case was solved.

"Coffee, Sheriff?" Trudy asked, handing her messages to her as she entered the office.

"Thanks, Trudy, but I just had some at home," Sharyn replied with a smile. "What are you doing in here on Sunday?"

"I thought you could use the extra hand what with this case and all. I'm going to church later, but I'll be back."

"I appreciate your help," Sharyn told her. She handed her the statement she'd taken from Tim Stryker the night before. "Maybe you could type this up for me."

"No problem, Sheriff," Trudy replied taking the handwritten copy from her.

Sharyn considered the words she'd given Trudy, thoughtfully. "I know I don't need to tell you how important it is that none of this leaks out yet."

"Nothing will leave here with me, Sheriff," Trudy assured her.

"Thanks, Trudy."

Sharyn walked into her office, wondering where Ernie was. The man was usually there with her from the time she walked into the office until the time she left.

"Tell me again what I get if you're right." A voice hailed her from her chair.

She closed her office door. "Where's Ernie?"

"I sent him out to buy you breakfast. I told him you were looking too thin."

"That's very thoughtful of you, Nick," she said caustically. "I didn't think you ever got out of bed until after ten."

"Is that the thanks I get for staying up most of the night reviewing your murder cases for you?"

Sharyn sat down in one of the chairs that faced her desk. "What have you got?"

"Let me show you," he replied tautly, switching on her computer. "I transferred everything to a disk for you. The files from ten years ago weren't in a computer file yet. I used the information from both cases, then had the computer program analyze and compare the data."

Sharyn came up behind him to look at the screen. "You weren't here yet when this happened, were you?"

"No," he answered, typing in his password, then loading the disk. "I remember everyone talking about the case when I started two years later. I think it was the worst murder Diamond Springs ever had to deal with."

"I'm sure you saw worse in New York," she replied as they waited for the disk to load.

He glanced back at her. "Is there something worse than an eighteen-year-old girl with her whole life in front of her having her life snuffed out?"

"No," she agreed, looking away from his intense gaze to the screen as the program came up.

"See here." He pointed to the screen as the results of the autopsies were compared by the computer. "There are so many similarities; you were right, Sharyn."

She was surprised by his use of her given name. In the almost two years they had worked together, he had never called her anything but Sheriff in his mocking, caustic tone. She didn't mention the fact, however, and kept her eyes glued to the screen.

"Here's a real kicker," Nick told her. "The gray lint material was found on Leila's body as well. There were no prints anywhere. Our boy was more careful, I guess. Ten years between murders could make you careless."

"Both girls were strangled with their pantyhose," Sharyn read from the screen. "The killer did the same thing both times. Put them back on but didn't touch them."

"Both girls were very similar in height and weight. Both girls had blond hair and blue eyes. Both girls were very accomplished and very popular. Neither girl was sexually assaulted during the murder. Both girls were found with flowers on their bodies and their dresses arranged neatly around them on the ground."

"Of course, the prom was a central theme between them," Sharyn considered. "Neither girl had anything under her nails that would suggest a fight. Neither girl was messed up at all, hair, make up, clothes."

"Both girls appeared to be struck down from behind by a blunt instrument. It was something small, though. Something hard and metal wielded with a lot of force, I think. There was only slight damage to the skull, and the mark was only about three or four inches wide, right at the base of the head. He wanted to knock them out. Not damage them."

"He must have had to catch them to keep them from hitting the pavement," Sharyn reflected.

"He might have refined his technique," Nick told

her. "Leila had a bruise on her knee as though she might have fallen to one knee when he hit her."

"Only one hit each time?" Sharyn wondered.

"One hit," he affirmed.

"Ed was right," Sharyn admitted. "The murders weren't identical."

Nick glanced at her. "Maybe not identical but too close to look the other way."

Sharyn looked at the last bit of information he'd put on the disk. It was pictures, side by side, of the dead girls. They were so alike, it was uncanny. She felt that weird shiver slide up her spine. Her impression at the parking lot may have been right.

"What are you going to do?" he questioned.

She let out a breath she had been holding without realizing it. "I'm not sure yet. I was waiting to make that decision based on your findings."

He looked at her in surprise. "Thanks. I didn't know you thought so highly of my work."

"I've always thought you are good at what you do," she answered him, surprised herself that he hadn't realized her good opinion of him.

"Whatever you do," he said, changing the subject, as he took the disk out of the computer, "it isn't going to be pleasant."

"I know." She sighed, recalling just the tip of that unpleasantness with her mother that morning. "It was my father who worked on that case ten years ago."

"He was a good man," Nick offered. "Everyone makes mistakes."

Sharyn could only hope other people would be as understanding. "Thanks for your help anyway."

"Is this where you kill me and hide my body to keep me from talking about the case?" he queried with a little more than his usual acerbic wit.

She looked at him. "I appreciate you keeping this between us." She held out her hand to him. He looked at it briefly, then took it in his own, giving it a mild squeeze. "We work well together. I hate to lose you, Nick."

He let go of her hand. "Sometimes things just don't work out."

"Is it something personal?" she wondered as he turned to walk out of her office.

"You might say that," he replied without turning back to her. "Good luck on the case."

Sharyn shook her head as he closed the door behind him. Whatever it was that was bothering him was something that he had to work out on his own. She didn't have time to speculate on his private life. She had a community to set back on its heels. And a double murder to solve.

Where was she going to start?

Ernie came in with her breakfast and a worried frown on his thin face. "You are looking a mite peaked."

"I'm fine," she told him briefly. "Sit down, Ernie. I have something to tell you."

She outlined the whole situation while she forced herself to eat the muffins and fruit he'd bought for her. At least he'd bought no-fat muffins, considering that the reunion was looming closer. That terrible green dress that everyone else loved so much was hanging somewhere, waiting for her.

"So, you're telling me that Ronnie Smith didn't murder Leila Bentley?"

"I don't think so," she replied.

"Who did?"

"Whoever murdered Carrie Sommers."

Ernie shook his head. "Before you jump to that conclusion, Sheriff, shouldn't you consider that it could be a copycat murder?"

"Ten years is a long time between crimes for a copycat," she stated.

"But not impossible," he argued, concerned about how this information would affect the town.

"Not impossible," she agreed reluctantly. "I just think the wrong man was blamed for the crime."

"Your daddy thought he was the right man," Ernie reminded her.

"I know."

"What are you going to do, Sheriff?"

"The only thing I know to do is reopen the Bentley investigation with an eye toward the two murders being committed by the same person."

Ernie whistled through his teeth and sat back in his chair. He respected Sharyn Howard as the sheriff, no matter what anyone else said. She'd done a good job in the time she'd been sheriff. But this was the first high profile case she'd had, and he didn't want her to lose the next election because of it.

"No one's gonna like it."

Sharyn smiled grimly. "That's putting it mildly, Ernie. I'm going to wait to do anything official until we hear Ed and Joe's reports from their interviews today and tomorrow. But if nothing changes, I'm going to reopen that investigation."

"What do you want me to do?" he asked, ready to support her in her decision if he couldn't talk her out of it.

"Thanks, Ernie. I need all the help I can get."

"Is that why Nick was here this morning?" he wondered.

She nodded. "I had him cross-checking the autopsy reports on both girls. That's what convinced me."

Ernie glanced at her. "You don't think he'd do something just to have the satisfaction of knowing you wouldn't be reelected, do you?"

Sharyn shook her head. "Nick and I may not get along, but I respect him as a professional, Ernie. He could have gone to the papers with it yesterday after I told him my suspicions. Whatever's wrong with

Nick is something personal. But I don't think it has anything to do with this investigation."

"Okay." He shrugged. "What now?"

"I'd appreciate it if you could get me all the information we have about Leila Bentley's murder. Newspaper clippings, interviews, everything. I'm going out to talk to the Sommerses again. They called again early this morning, and they want to talk to me whether I can get the information from someone else or not."

"You don't want me to come out with you?" he asked, just a little hurt to be left behind.

"I need you to get this other information for me, Ernie," she told him.

"Yes, ma'am."

"Thanks. I'll be back later."

Ernie went to start looking up those files from the archives. But he ordered lunch for the sheriff first. It was going to be a long day.

Cara Sommers was red-eyed but lucid when Sharyn arrived at their home. The grieving parents greeted her together in the foyer, then led her into the library where they sat beside a blazing fire in a large stone fireplace.

"Thank you for coming, Sheriff," Carrie's mother began. "I'm sorry I fell apart yesterday, but it was just so unexpected."

Sharyn nodded and twisted her hat in her hand. "Don't worry about it, Mrs. Sommers. I would like to tell you how much all of us regret the loss of your daughter."

The other woman glanced at her husband. "We appreciate it, Sheriff. I just wanted to tell you that I knew what time Carrie left here Friday night. She left about six-thirty because she was on the dance committee. She and Tim drove separately to the dance because of their plans for later in the evening. But I had them both come here, so that I could take pictures of Carrie coming down the stairway in her gown and the two of them getting ready to go."

"I spoke with Tim yesterday when he got back from the beach," Sharyn told her.

Mr. Sommers had the grace to look ashamed. "I'm sorry about what I said to him, Sheriff. I was angry, I guess. I called him this morning and apologized. The one thing we don't need to do right now is hurt each other."

"That was for the best," Sharyn told him, relieved that he had managed to figure it out on his own.

"I was so excited," Cara Sommers told her. "I went out and had the film developed at the one-hour processor." She handed Sharyn some pictures.

Sharyn looked at the smiling face of the girl she had only seen dead in that cold parking lot. She and Tim were clowning for the camera, putting on his boutonniere and her corsage. The corsage was clearly made of the same flowers that she had been holding. "May I keep these?"

"Yes, please; I had copies made for the family."

"Thanks, Mrs. Sommers."

"Sheriff," the woman said, catching Sharyn's hand with her icy cold one. "Catch the person who did this to my baby girl. Tell us what we can do. My husband is going to offer a reward. Don't let this person hurt anyone else."

Sharyn took hold of the woman's hand. "I will, Mrs. Sommers. I promise you, I will."

Sharyn drove back from the Sommers' house the long way. The road wound past the old Diamond Springs Presbyterian church that had been built in 1784. The tiny church was still in use with its hardwood benches and balcony that ran around the outer edge of the sanctuary.

She remembered sitting in that balcony, listening to the sermon with her parents and later her younger sister, Kristie. Lanterns hung from the rafters, electric now, but exact replicas of the ones used when the church had been built. It was a small, closely knit congregation that knew the name of every child that fidgeted and the color of every woman's hat. They still had the minister to dinner on Sunday evenings and had picnics on the grounds surrounding the church.

She got out of her car, thinking about how long it had been since she'd been to church. Almost two years since her father had died and she had attended his funeral.

There had been so many people that day, under the spreading oaks, that cars had to be parked down the road for a mile. It had been summer and the trees were in full leaf, whispering softly behind the minister's head as he read the sermon before they buried her father.

He had been killed in a botched robbery attempt at the local convenience store. He had been running for sheriff that year, and the would-be robbers recognized his face as he bought a gallon of milk. He wasn't wearing his gun or his uniform. They shot him down and fled with the fifty dollars in cash they'd taken from the store.

They'd caught the two boys who'd killed him. They were teenagers from another county. They were in prison in Raleigh, along with Leila Bentley's murderer.

Sharyn had run for her father's office after his death. Some people said that she won because of the huge sympathy vote. She didn't care. If her performance in office wasn't good, they could vote her out again in two years. But she was going to try hard to be a good sheriff. As good as her father had been.

She found her father's grave. He was buried next to his father and his mother. All of the past ten generations of Howards were buried there. Someday, Sharyn knew she would lie there beside them.

"Hi, Dad," she said, brushing the dead leaves and

debris from his grave. She sat down on the cold stone bench beneath the little weeping willow they'd planted. She looked out at the old oaks, still leafless in the cold weather. The smaller trees might be fooled by the sunny days, but it took longer to convince the oaks.

"You know, I wouldn't do anything to take away from what you did when you were alive. But this case is wrong. I can feel it. I'm not saying you didn't do the best you could at the time. But I'm looking at another murder, and I think you got the wrong man."

The wind blew icy crystals down from the Uwharries that she could see in the distance. "I have to do this, Dad. I wouldn't be doing my job if I didn't. I'd like to think you'd have done the same thing with one of Grampa's cases, if it came up this way. I know you would've wanted me to do what was right anyway. It never mattered to you if you stepped on a few toes to do it."

An owl hooted from somewhere in the cemetery, and the rain started falling a little harder. Not a good sign, she supposed, but maybe a sign of things to come.

Chapter Four

They met in the interrogation room on Monday morning, sitting around the big wooden table. Sharyn had called Nick in to present his findings on the autopsy. She wanted to hear all of their opinions on the Sommers case, as well as the advent of re-opening the Bentley case. Although she was pretty sure how that was going to go.

Ed had been able to speak with most of Carrie's teachers, including the chaperones for the dance.

"There were three teachers involved with the prom. They worked on it from decorations to cleanup. They left together." He consulted his notebook. "Between one-thirty and two A.M. They weren't sure of the exact time. The prom was over between twelve-thirty and one A.M. Cleanup took about an hour for their part. The principal was out of town that night, but the vice principal was there. He said the dance was quiet, no problems. None of them has ever heard any sort of threat against Carrie. She was a good student, dependable, well liked. None of them recall whether Carrie's car was in the parking lot when they left. One teacher, Mrs. Markham, feels pretty sure that it was. Apparently some of the students left their cars in the lot and picked them up later anyway, so there was more than just Carrie's car there."

"Were they leaving her to lock up after they left?" Sharyn asked, looking over his report.

"No, there's a custodian." He checked his notes again. "David Mauney. I spoke with him. He said he was fishing down at the lake until about two A.M. because he had to wait to finish the cleanup until then. He walked up from the lake and went in through the back of the school. He cleaned up until about four A.M., then got in his car and went home."

"Any cars there besides Carrie's?"

"He said he thought there were several cars there, but he wasn't sure whose any of them were. One of them could have been Carrie's. He wouldn't have known the difference."

Sharyn sighed. "All right, thanks, Ed. Joe?"

"I spoke with most of her friends. Most of them were back yesterday. Some went farther than the beach after the prom, or no one was sure where they were, so I haven't talked to them. Everyone I talked to felt the same way about her. She was a wonderful person, well liked and involved in everything. Three of the girls were on the dance committee with her. They left around the same time as the teachers left that night. Again, because of the other cars parked in the lot, no one is really sure that they saw Carrie's car. They just assumed it must have been there."

"And no one thought to wait and see if everyone left safely," Ed reflected with a shake of his head. "They just flew out of there without thinking."

"Comes from living in a small town where safety isn't a big factor," Ernie added.

"Comes from a sad lack of education about their own safety," Nick told them. "Small town or not, they should know better."

"So something happened to Carrie between the school and the car. As far as everyone knows, she left the school with everyone else. They expected her to just get in her car and drive away as they had, but something stopped her."

"Some*one* stopped her," Joe said. "And I don't think it was one of her little friends."

"No jealous ex-boyfriends?"

"She only dated one other boy. That was two years ago. He moved to Charleston."

"Are we sure about that? He's not skulking around somewhere?" Ernie wondered, hoping that the sheriff wouldn't have to present her theory.

"Nope. He's enrolled at the Citadel. We even know where he was Friday night and Saturday morning. I don't think he was pining for the girl," Joe told him.

"What about Tim Stryker?" Ed queried.

Sharyn shook her head. "I didn't get any feeling from him that he was anything but devastated, and it would have taken a major plotting event for him to have been with his friends at parties and manage to slip away, murder Carrie, then go back."

"The car was clean," Ernie determined.

"Except for the gray wool fibers that matched those found on the girl's body," Sharyn agreed. "The hood wasn't latched, but I suppose that could have been an oversight on her part. Nothing else seems to go along with that."

"The grounds were clear. Except for the rest of the corsage in the dumpster and the gray fibers." Ed wrestled with trying to piece it together.

"That leaves us with someone outside the school. Probably someone she didn't know," Joe surmised. "A sick someone."

"Great." Ed closed his file. "The press is gonna love that."

Sharyn glanced at Nick, then sat forward in her chair. "I'm afraid it means more than that."

"What do you mean?" Ed asked quickly. "Is there something else?"

"It must have something to do with Nick." Ed

frowned. "He looks like the cat who swallowed the canary."

"Nick," she said reluctantly. "I'd like you to present your findings."

"All right," he agreed. "Would you like me to start with Carrie? Or Leila?"

Ed groaned and Joe pushed his chair away from the table. He got up and crossed to the window.

"What's this all about, Sheriff?" Ed demanded.

"You'll have to hear me out on this," she told them.

"You were still in school when it happened," Joe replied. "How can you know so much about it?"

"When you hear the autopsy report on both girls, you'll understand," she argued.

Nick presented both cases clearly and quickly. Joe took his seat again and both men listened quietly, but they were clearly unconvinced by the evidence.

"If you're looking for a connection between the two cases, that could do it," Ed said. "If you take them one at a time, they're as alike as any other two cases."

"They're the same in some ways, Sheriff, but they're different, too." Joe tried to convince her.

Sharyn faced them silently for a long moment, looking at their mutinous faces. She respected these men. They had been on the job much longer than her almost two years. They had experience that she didn't have, but she also felt that they were wrong in this case.

"I think you're letting your prejudices about going over this case again affect your judgment," she told them finally. "How many homicides do we have in Diamond Springs in a year?"

"One or two," Joe replied. "Mostly domestic violence cases gone bad."

"And out of the cases you've investigated in the past twenty years, how many of them have had these characteristics? The two girls were nearly identical in height and weight. Same hair. Same eyes. They were both killed in the same parking lot after a prom. They were both strangled with their pantyhose after being hit from behind in a single blow that probably rendered them unconscious. They were both laid out like they were being tucked in for the night and neither one was sexually assaulted. Nothing was stolen. The cars were still sitting there, and the keys were in the girls' purses."

Ed scribbled on a blank piece of paper in front of him. Joe looked out the window. The room was silent between them.

"Saying there's a connection between these two murders implies that the killer or killers has been here for the past ten years," Nick spoke into the quiet room. "No one likes that idea."

"It makes me feel like a fool," Ed told them bluntly. "I worked on that case with your father."

"I was there, too," Ernie added, looking at both men. "I don't like it either."

"But you'd do anything to make the sheriff happy," Joe said sharply.

Ernie looked away, his mouth tense and his hands balled into fists.

Joe relented. "I'm sorry, Ernie. That was uncalled for. It's just this case." He turned to the sheriff. "Are you sure you know what you're doing with this? Maybe you don't remember how bad it was when it first happened. If you tell everyone that the killer is still on the loose and has killed another girl, we're gonna have a panic."

"I'm not proposing that we tell everyone what's going on," she suggested since the fireworks seemed to have subsided. "It might get around anyway, but if we're careful, we can keep it quiet. Maybe we can surprise whoever did this. You know he must feel secure. It's been ten years, and he hasn't been caught. How would he get caught this time?"

Ed shook his head. "So, where do we start?"

"Ernie's making up files for all of us about the Bentley case. I already have some of the information. It's been ten years. Some of the original witnesses are gone. We're going to have to locate them and start all over."

"Old Mr. Belmont was principal then," Joe said. "He's been dead for a few years."

"I want to cross-reference between the two cases:

which teachers are still here and are there suspects who were questioned in the first case who might be worth looking at in the second. Let's find all the similarities first and hope that they lead us to something else."

"This isn't going to stay a secret for long," Ernie told her. "Once people get an idea of what you're doing, the fat's gonna be in the fire."

Sharyn refused to comment and turned to Nick. "Any way I could get you to check out those gray cotton fibers? If they are from gloves, maybe we can isolate where they came from."

"No problem," he answered with a quick nod of his dark head.

"What about us?" Ed asked, straightening his tan shirt and belt.

"I appreciate your cooperation on this, all of you. I know this won't be easy, but maybe we can catch a killer before he gets another ten years to do it again."

Ed and Joe nodded. Joe nudged Ernie, who was sitting, stone-faced beside him. "Come on, let me buy you a cup of coffee."

"Ed, I want you working the teachers again. Joe, the students. Ernie will work up lists for both of you. Let's find out who's still here after ten years. But let's try to keep this as quiet as we can for as long as we can. Don't lie about the investigation but dodge the truth as much as possible. I think you're right. This could cause a lot of people to worry more than is necessary. After all, the man has only killed two women in ten years, and both of them were nearly identical."

"Unless he shifts his interest," Ernie suggested.

Sharyn nodded grimly. "Let's hope that doesn't happen."

Ed and Joe walked out with Ernie between them, trying to tease him out of his anger over Joe's careless remark.

"You must be one of the bravest people I know," Nick stated flatly when they were alone.

She looked up at him. "Thanks. I guess."

He glanced at her. "It's not going to be easy for you, you know. You're gonna take a lot of heat for this, even if it works out to be true and you catch the killer."

"Yeah, but if I'm right and we do catch the killer, all that heat is gonna feel like a summer shower."

He smiled. "I guess so. Good luck, anyway."

"Thanks."

Sharyn took her files into her office, wondering at Nick's change of attitude. He was usually surly, sarcastic and generally hard to get along with. Maybe the fact that he was leaving made him more amenable.

"Where are you headed in all this mess?" Ernie asked, coming into her office a few minutes later.

"I'm going up to Raleigh to see Ronnie Smith."

He drew in a sharp breath. "You'll want some company."

She nodded. "If you can finish those files on your laptop in the car . . ."

"You know it, ma'am."

"Ernie," she said for the hundredth time. "I wish you'd call me Sharyn."

He shook his head. "That wouldn't be right, ma'am. Just let me get that laptop and my jacket."

They rode together in easy silence while Sharyn thought about the case, and Ernie's fingers tapped on the keyboard.

"What made my father so sure that Ronnie Smith killed Leila?" she asked him as the patrol car ate up the miles between Diamond Springs and Raleigh. The sun was shining brightly, even though the temperature was chilly. Traffic was light on the highway.

Ernie thought back to that time ten years earlier. "Ronnie was living here temporarily, working as a construction worker on the new power plant. He was drunk that night. He'd tried to assault Leila at the pool room the night before."

"Assault her?" she asked.

"Leila had been waiting for—I can't recall her boyfriend's name. Apparently he was paying for a table for them. Ronnie Smith was drunk and walked up to her, gave her a hard time. Tried to kiss her or something. She slapped him. Her boyfriend and his school friends took him out and gave him a beating."

Sharyn had to admit that it sounded pretty convincing. If she had something like that for Carrie's homicide, she would have looked that way as well.

"I was with your father when he went to pick Smith up. The boy was drunk, didn't know where he'd been the night before. No one had seen him or could vouch for him. And he admitted that he wanted to get back at Leila and her boyfriend."

"So much for motive and opportunity," she agreed. "What about the murder itself?"

Ernie shrugged. "We knew about the fibers, but the coroner identified them as coming from his coat."

"How did he account for the lack of fingerprints?"

"Gloves," Ernie suggested. "We found a pair of work gloves that were entered into evidence, and the coroner testified at the trial that he thought the initial blow could have come from the flat of a hammer. Smith's hammer was clean, but we considered that he had cleaned it after the murder since he had to use it for work the next day."

"All of that makes sense," Sharyn responded. "It makes a convincing case."

Ernie started typing again. "I know. We were all convinced that he did the crime. Maybe we were just too convinced."

"But without this second murder," she concluded, "why would you have thought anything else?"

The big gray form of the prison began to unfold as they slowed down for the entrance. A guard checked them through. Sharyn left her gun at the front office. Ernie never carried a weapon. They were ushered into the warden's office, a sparse box with heavy dark furniture and several monitors that showed areas around the prison.

"What can I do for you, Sheriff?" he asked when they had been seated.

"I'd like the opportunity to talk with Ronald Smith," she told him. Ernie quoted his prison number so that the warden could locate him in the system.

"Death row," the stocky man on the other side of the desk stated. "We don't encourage visitors at this stage, Sheriff."

"I understand," Sharyn answered. "But I may be reopening the investigation into the murder he's charged with. There's evidence to suggest that he might not have been responsible for the crime."

The warden looked up from his monitor. "Really? I hope that's more than just a supposition on your part, Sheriff. This man is scheduled to die next week unless the governor issues a last-minute reprieve, which, frankly, I don't look for."

Sharyn smiled pleasantly. "All the more reason

for me to move along with this investigation, Warden. If I'm right, it could mean this man's life."

He frowned, then nodded his head. "All right. I'll go along with this. It won't be the first time someone gave a man false hope. Good luck, Sheriff." He stood up and offered Sharyn his hand.

"Thank you, Warden."

Sharyn and Ernie were escorted to the visitation area. They stood, waiting, while Ronnie Smith was brought from death row.

"Nice guy," Ernie remarked softly, looking at the myriad of cameras that surrounded them.

"Be careful what you say," she warned him. "I'm sure he could hear you breathe if he wanted to."

"This place always gives me the creeps," he confided. "I visited my father once here when I was a child. Never forgot it."

Sharyn stared at him. "Your father was in prison?"

He grimaced and looked away. "It's not something I want to talk about, Sheriff."

Before she could answer, two burly guards escorted a tall, lanky man with graying hair and a flat face into the room. He was dressed in a prison jumpsuit, and there were chains around his feet. His hands were cuffed together. He shuffled to a chair at a small gray table and sat down. He didn't look up at them.

Sharyn and Ernie came to sit at the other two

chairs. The guards stood off to the side, but it was impossible not be aware of their presence. What must it be like, Sharyn considered, to live this way twenty-four hours a day? It seemed as though death would have to be a release.

"Hello, Ronnie," Sharyn began when the man didn't look up or speak. "I'm the sheriff of Diamond Springs, Sharyn Howard. I've come to ask you a few questions about what happened ten years ago."

"Howard?" He picked up on the name and raised his head to look at her. "Are you related to the Sheriff Howard who sent me here?"

"I'm his daughter," she admitted.

"You don't look much like him," he said quietly.

Sharyn resisted the urge to push back her curly copper hair. "I know."

"Where is he?" Ronnie wondered in a voice as devoid of inflection as was possible.

"He was killed two years ago," she told him. "He was shot during a robbery." She was prepared for him to gloat over the fact. It made her stomach tense up and her hands fasten down hard on her pen, but she didn't look away from him.

"That's too bad," he replied finally. "He wasn't really a bad guy."

"Thanks," she replied tautly. "I came to talk about you, Ronnie." She looked closely into his pale blue eyes. "I'm reopening the investigation into the murder."

He didn't blink. "Why?"

Sharyn looked away, glancing at the guard to her right and back again. "I believe we have evidence that someone else killed Leila Bentley."

If she had expected a response from him, excitement, bewilderment, anger, she was disappointed. He simply stared at her with those disinterested blue eyes. He looked like a man who knew that he was going to die and had accepted it. Nothing mattered.

Sharyn and Ernie exchanged glances, then Sharyn looked back at Ronnie.

"I wanted to ask you a few questions about what happened."

"It's all in the record," he told her.

"I know," she replied. "I guess I was hoping there might be something else that you could tell me."

He nodded and his gaze flitted around the room as though he were trying to recall. "I met her at the pool hall. She was so gorgeous, you know? Like a model. She looked at me with those big blue eyes and that sweet pink mouth. I thought she wanted me, you know? She was standing there all alone. I was drunk, I guess. And I wanted her. I thought that maybe she wanted me too. I was wrong."

"What happened then?" she asked.

"Her boyfriend came out of the back. He started to push me around, and I slapped him. He was just a punk, you know? Then he went and got some of his friends. It took five of them to hurt me. I remember looking over at her in the streetlight, and she looked like she was sorry."

"Leila?"

"Yeah. I didn't even know what her name was until the cops came for me the next day. She was hot, you know?"

Sharyn nodded. "What did you do then?"

"I went back to the motel where I was staying. There was a girl hanging around there. We had a good time. I guess I got drunker after that, thinking about Leila. Wishing it had been her instead of that other girl. I don't remember anything after that."

"Do you think that you killed Leila, Ronnie?" Sharyn wondered.

He looked at her blandly. "I don't know. I've never really hurt anyone. I mean we'd mix it up after work, you know? But I never hit a woman. I just don't remember."

Sharyn digested the information, going over it again in her mind, wondering what it was about what he'd said that bothered her. She finally shook her head and gathered her folder.

"I don't know what's going to happen with this," she told him. "I'm going to talk with someone about delaying your sentence until the investigation is complete. I can't make any promises."

He shrugged. "That's okay. It used to bother me, but it doesn't anymore. I'm used to it, you know?"

Sharyn stood up and took his hand. The guards at the sides of the room moved quickly toward them. "Good-bye, Ronnie," she told him, squeezing his hand. "I'll do the best I can for you."

"Thanks." His hand was limp and cold in her own, as though he were already dead. His eyes moved to her face. "You're a good person, like your old man, I guess. I think they made him do this to me. He didn't have a choice, you know?"

"They?" she asked curiously.

"It doesn't matter," he answered. The guards took his arms and moved him towards the door. "Good-bye, Sheriff."

Ernie and Sharyn didn't exchange another word with one another until they were back in the patrol car and the gray prison walls were fading behind them.

"What do you think?" Ernie asked finally.

"Was that what he told my father?" Sharyn asked, taking a deep breath.

Ernie nodded. "Pretty much. As far as I can recall. He's saying what he said at the trial."

"And it convinced people that he was guilty," she replied thoughtfully. "I can see how a jury wouldn't be overly excited about the man. He's pretty pathetic."

"I think it was that he didn't know," Ernie told her. "He was drunk and he had made a pass at Leila. He fought with her boyfriend. It seemed to all fit together. I remember talking it over with your father."

"There's something about it that bothers me," Sharyn told him, not taking her eyes from the road as it twisted homeward into the coming twilight.

"It's probably because you're already thinking that way," Ernie suggested. "You were pretty sure he was innocent before you came up here."

"Are you saying I've lost my objectivity?" she questioned with a faint smile on her face.

"No," he assured her, a little flustered, then backtracked. "Yes, I guess I am."

"You might be right," she agreed. "I wouldn't reopen this case if I didn't believe that there were to many similarities to be coincidence."

Ernie smiled and attacked his keyboard. "You know, you could be wrong."

"I suppose so."

They drove on and Ernie began working on his laptop again. Sharyn switched on the headlights as they passed a billboard advertising swimwear. The giant-sized, spotlit couple was frolicking on a beach. His hands were on her waist as she laughed up at him. Their faces were close together.

"That's it!" she said, hitting her hand on the steering wheel as she pulled over to the side of the road. She stared up at the big sign and its happy occupants.

"What?" he wondered, shocked that she had pulled over.

"The one thing that Ronnie made clear from the beginning. He wanted Leila in the worst way. He wouldn't have just folded her hands and made her dress pretty. He would have touched her, Ernie. That's what's been bothering me."

Chapter Five

Ernie shook his head. "You might as well go on, Sheriff."

"What do you mean?" she wondered, starting the car back on the road.

"I mean, that was one of the things that the defense attorney said in the trial. He wanted her. Why didn't he assault her?"

Sharyn digested his words. "So, what was the answer?"

"The state had a doctor testify that he was probably too drunk to be able to do what he really wanted to do to her."

"But he wasn't too drunk to be able to lay her out like a beauty queen?" Sharyn demanded smartly.

Ernie shrugged, not looking up from his keyboard. "That's what they said. Don't shoot the messenger."

"That doesn't make sense, Ernie," she replied logically. She glanced at him when he didn't answer. "Or do you see the sense it makes?"

"At the time, it made sense," he told her quietly. "We did the best we could. Maybe now, looking at a copy of the original, you can see some things that we didn't. Doesn't mean we didn't look at it."

Sharyn glanced at him. "I didn't mean to sound like I was criticizing, Ernie. I remember what it was like after Leila's death. My dad didn't sleep at home for a month. My mom cried all the time."

He nodded but didn't say anything else until they reached the office. He packed up his computer and smiled at her. "Sometimes, its easier to see what's already been done," he reminded her. "Hindsight is always twenty-twenty."

"I know," she agreed. "I'm sorry, Ernie. I didn't mean for you to take offense."

"I didn't," he replied. "I'll see you tomorrow, Sheriff."

Sharyn drove home, thinking about Ernie. The man never got upset over anything she said or did, unless it was not eating or forgetting her raincoat. He was always a sounding board for her ideas, without getting personally involved.

It just showed her the extent to which case reached. If it bothered Ernie, how much would everyone else be bothered by it? When she finally had to admit that she was reopening the case, anything could happen. Ed and Joe had gone along with the idea, but, short of resigning, what else could they do?

She parked the car in front of the garage and wondered why all of the lights were on in the formal living room. Her mother never entertained ordinary folks there. Grimacing, she let herself into the kitchen, hoping it wasn't Aunt Selma wanting to work on that terrible green dress. She didn't think she could stand on the footstool and be poked and prodded while her aunt and her mother told her how the color made her eyes look pretty, and the style was so flattering to her full figure.

Sharyn had made it past the door that led to the formal living room. She didn't dare breathe as she opened her bedroom door and prepared to close it behind her and lock it.

"Sharyn?" her mother called out, walking out of the living room.

"I'm exhausted, Mom," Sharyn told her without preamble. "I don't think I can do anything else tonight."

"We have a guest who wants to talk to you," Faye Howard told her daughter. "He's been waiting for a while. I think you owe him the courtesy of speaking with him."

"Who is it?" Sharyn hissed at her mother.

Faye Howard looked at her daughter and turned back into the living room. Sharyn knew then that her mother was responsible for whoever it was being there. She put her hat down on the bed, took off her holster and gun, then raked a hand through her curls. She looked at her freckled face closely in the mirror, wondering if having an enormous amount of freckles indicated a stubborn, troublesome nature, as her aunt had once told her.

Sharyn glanced at her mother, then at their guest as she walked into the living room. Caison Talbot. She should have known.

"Senator." She greeted the old family friend. "How are you?"

"Worried," he admitted, standing up from the plastic-covered gold sofa. "I'm worried, Sharyn. Do you know why?"

Sharyn looked at her mother, who looked away from her intent stare. "I can only assume that my mother told you that I was about to reopen the Leila Bentley murder case. Is that right?"

Caison Talbot shook his white mane of hair. He was a lion of a man, tall and broad-shouldered. Even in his late sixties, he was formidable. When she was a child, Sharyn had actually been frightened of him.

"Your mother did the right thing, young lady. What do you think you're doing, stirring up that old memory again? Wasn't it terrible enough the first time?"

Sharyn held her shoulders back and her head high as her mother had been trying to get her to do since she was ten years old. "I believe there may have been a mistake, Senator. I don't think Ronnie Smith was the murderer."

"Because of this new murder?" He stared her down. "I think the new sheriff just has a case of stage fright. This is your first homicide investigation. You should expect to feel uneasy."

"That's not what's wrong, Senator. I think all of you did the best you could at the time, but this murder proves that the man who was responsible for Leila's death is still here. Maybe he hasn't made a move in ten years. Maybe he won't make a move again in his lifetime. But an innocent man is in prison and may die for that crime. Ronnie Smith didn't kill Leila Bentley."

The senator knew bluster when he heard it. Hadn't he invented it? "You know I was the prosecutor in that case."

"I know," she admitted. "You ran for Congress on the strength of that conviction. But that was ten years ago. Surely you aren't worried about it having any effect on your constituents for another election?"

He shook his head. "Don't you preach to me, young woman! I used to help your daddy change your drawers! No one knows what's going to affect the voters, least of all you. You've only won one election, and the way you're going, you won't win another."

"If you're telling me that I can't win an election unless I roll over and pretend that I don't know when something's wrong, then I won't win the next election, and I don't care. Don't you understand? The person who killed Leila is still out there. He killed again. Doesn't that mean anything to you?"

Caison Emmet Talbot stood up to his full, impressive height, towering over Sharyn, his white hair spread around his florid face like a fury. "You're asking for trouble, girl. More trouble than you can handle. Drop it now, before the press gets wind of it. Solve this case for yourself. Don't make yourself look like a fool!"

He nodded to Faye Howard, who walked him to the front door. Sharyn left the living room without saying another word and closed her bedroom door behind her.

The next morning she was up and out before her mother had left her room. She drove to the school and stepped out of the car. The morning was cold. Her breath was frosty in the air before her. She pushed her hands into her coat pockets and walked through the school grounds.

Was she wrong?

She recalled Leila's death and the awful aftermath that attacked the town. People had wanted to hang Ronnie Smith in the town square. She couldn't pretend that it hadn't affected her, too. Graduation had been a tearful good-bye to the beautful prom queen. The town had hung black banners as they usually hung Christmas wreaths in December. No one could believe that something so terrible could have happened in Diamond Springs.

Somehow, it made it seem better that the man who was responsible wasn't from there. People were able to look at it as an isolated event. Of course, no one from the town could have done such a hideous thing. It was the price they paid for having to invite strangers into their quiet lives.

Sharyn recalled seeing the pictures of her father, Caison Talbot and the rest of the deputies in the paper. George Albert had been the presiding judge in the case. They were the heroes who had delivered Diamond Springs from the forces of darkness. They were the good standing against the bad of the world. People were in awe of them.

Thinking about it, she realized what a tormented time that must have been for George. He'd been a hero in his professional life, but it was about that time that he and Brenda had made the decision to send Richard away.

She'd always wondered what prompted the decision. Richard had always been a wild child. It was only a few days after Leila's death when she heard that he was gone. She'd been so involved in the grief and shock surrounding the other girl's death that she hadn't spared much time to think about Richard. It seemed to her that Brenda and George could forgive their son anything. What had been so bad that it finally was too much?

She shook her head to clear it. Richard coming home was the least of her problems.

It had haunted her that she had been one of the last people to see Leila alive. For months she'd had nightmares about the other girl being tortured and killed. For years, kids had spoken about seeing Leila's ghost prowling the school grounds at night. She had nearly become a legend in Diamond Springs.

But it wasn't as though Sharyn had walked around for the past ten years feeling that they had arrested the wrong man. It had only been when she had seen Carrie's young body in her pretty prom dress that she felt that it had to be the work of the same person. Meeting Ronnie Smith certainly hadn't convinced her of his innocence. It was easy to see why her father and the jury thought that he did the original crime.

The school grounds were quiet yet. School wouldn't be in session for another few hours.

Sharyn remembered going to school there. She hadn't been beautiful or accomplished like Leila or Carrie. She'd been stubborn and angry. Leaving Diamond Springs to go to college in Chapel Hill had been the best move of her life. Away from everything she knew, she began to experience life, and she had blossomed. When she had finally come back, she had enough self-confidence to overcome anything. Or at least she had felt that way until her father's death.

Fog rose like a cloud from the lake that was just visible behind the trees. For as long as the school had been there, the high school students had gone swimming in the last hot days of school. It wasn't allowed, of course, but there had always been a way to do it anyway. Sharyn had done it once, dressed in her jeans and a t-shirt. When she had walked out of the water, the school guidance counselor had been there, waiting for her. Her mother had cried when she was suspended for a day. Her father had shaken his head and wouldn't look at her.

I know I'm right.

There was just that feeling, that slight tingling sensation in the pit of her stomach that told her that Ronnie Smith wasn't Leila's killer. He or she, probably he, was still out there. He had killed again. Whatever had motivated him to kill Leila had hit him again with Carrie. It was probably frightening after ten long years to have killed again. The surge of fear that you might get caught after so long. But something about Carrie had pushed him over the edge again.

As she passed the stand of trees, a movement caught her eye. It was fast and furtive.

Drawing her gun, she followed it to the shore. There were boat skid marks along the shoreline where people had pulled up their boats to fish or swim. The lake was foggy, obscuring the mountains on the other side of the water.

She put away her gun and looked across the water. A small boat was floating away from the shore. A large man in a green jacket was hunched down in the bow. He looked back at her with wild dark eyes his dark hair flat against his head.

"Hello . . . hello. . . ." she called out. Her voice echoed back to her as the boat floated into a fog bank.

Sharyn shivered and started back out of the trees towards the school. She couldn't be *sure* who it was. This had been a safe place for her as a teen. She remembered swimming off a nearby pier in the summer, looking at the school in the distance and dreading the end of vacation.

The dark figure was a frightening specter.

As she walked from the lake to the tennis courts, she recognized the school principal, Mr. Strauss, along with another man who was dressed in overalls, coming toward her.

"Sheriff." Mr. Strauss nodded to her. "This is Mr. Mauney, our groundskeeper and custodian."

"Mr. Mauney." Shayrn acknowledged him. "What can I do for you?"

"We were just wondering that about you, Sheriff," Mr. Strauss told her nervously. "Nothing else has happened, has it?"

"No," she told him, smiling at the groundskeeper as well. The man scowled back at her. The investigation's probably been keeping him busy, she considered. "I was just looking around."

"The deputies have gone over everything," the principal hastened to assure her as she continued walking. "We've been more than cooperative."

"And we certainly appreciate that," she replied, wishing the man would go away.

"Do you have any leads?" he wondered nervously.

"We're working on the information that we have so far," she answered naturally. "I can't really give out that information yet."

"Of course, of course," he added quickly. "If there's anything either one of us can do, please let us know."

"I will," she answered. "Thanks for your cooperation."

The custodian put his head down and started to walk away.

"Mr. Mauney." She called him back while the principal made a hasty retreat.

"What is it, Sheriff? You know I'm a busy man."

"I appreciate that," she told him, used to people wanting to brush her aside. "I'd like to ask you a few questions. It won't take long."

He walked back to her side, a strong limp in his right leg. "I already answered questions for the deputies."

"I know, and I appreciate your helping me out," she said with a smile. "I think I remember you being here when I went to school."

He looked at her closely. "I don't remember you."

She glanced down at the ground. "I suppose I wasn't particularly memorable. Weren't you in the Vietnam war?"

He nodded. "I fought for three years over there until I took some shrapnel, and they sent me home. Not that anybody appreciated what I did."

"I think we can all appreciate the sacrifice you made," she told him. "Do you remember the murder that happened here ten years ago?"

"I was only working here part time back then, before John Belmont died. I remember all the fuss that they made. And the cleanup."

"Mind if I ask you where you were the night of Carrie Sommers' murder?" she queried, squinting into a shaft of bright sunlight that had escaped the cloud cover.

"I was fishing down at the lake," he replied quietly. "Waiting for the prom to be over so I could clean up."

"What time did you get back to the school?"

He rolled his eyes. "Is this necessary, Sheriff? "

She smiled again. "I'm afraid I ask everybody these questions, Mr. Mauney. Nothing personal."

"I'm not sure." He shrugged. "I guess I got back around one-thirty or two A.M. Everybody was gone."

"What about Carrie's car?"

"I park on the other side of the school. I didn't come out on this side. I worked and got things cleaned up, and I went home."

"What time was that?" she asked.

"What difference does it make?"

Sharyn sighed. "I have to fill out these reports."

"I don't know," he growled. "My wife was home. She'll vouch for me."

"There's nothing to vouch for," she said carefully. She put out her hand. "Thanks for your time."

He looked at her hand, then turned away and limped back inside the school.

Sharyn looked at her gloved hand as well but there wasn't anything to see but black wool. The man wasn't particularly friendly. She had been hoping he would have some answers that might help her link the past killing with the present one. Obviously, she had been mistaken.

But she felt fortified against her own doubts that she was chasing ghosts in the case. She was going with her feeling that the cases were connected. She wasn't going to let Caison Talbot scare her off.

Knowing it wouldn't do any good to try to talk

to Caison about Leila's murder, she had tracked down the lawyer who had done the defense work for Ronnie Smith. He had been a public defender ten years before, just starting out, but now he was a partner in a law firm. Obviously the case hadn't hurt him either. He had his law office in Charlotte, and he agreed to see her that day.

The drive into Charlotte was hectic as always and she got lost somewhere around Queens Road. Carefully, Sharyn retraced her path back down Queens Road, and this time she found the large red brick building on the corner. With a sense of relief, she parked the patrol car and walked inside. She left her hat in the car, not worried that she wouldn't appear official enough. The sun had come out. It was warm on the top of her head, and the wind blew past her face with a light caress.

"Sheriff Howard." Mike Dakin stood up to take her hand as his secretary showed her into his office. "It's nice to meet you. I read about the recent murder in Diamond Springs. That's a tragedy for someone so young. I have children of my own; I can empathize with the girl's parents."

Sharyn shook his hand, then took a seat in front of the glass and chrome desk. "It is a terrible thing," she agreed.

"Howard?" he wondered at her name. "Are you related to the sheriff who was in Diamond Springs ten years ago?"

She nodded. "He was my father. He was killed in a robbery two years ago."

"I'm sorry," the well-dressed lawyer added uncomfortably. "What can I do for you, Sheriff?"

"I've come about the Leila Bentley case. I believe you were the defense lawyer for Ronnie Smith?"

"Yeah." He shook his head and shuffled some papers on his desk. "That was a mess."

"How so?"

He looked past her and frowned. "I was young, just starting out. The man had no alibi and wouldn't do much of anything to help himself. Everyone was so sure that he was the killer. I tried to get the case moved to another county, but the judge refused to change a thing. He said he felt Smith could get a fair trial in Diamond Springs, but there was just no way."

Sharyn took a deep breath. "Did you feel as though he were guilty?"

Mike Dakin looked at her intently. "He was a wall crawler, I'll grant you that, but a murderer? I don't think so. He didn't know where he'd been or what he'd done. It just made him a prime target to get the case over with as quickly as possible. Nobody wanted it to hang around."

"I read that you raised a question about why he hadn't violated the girl if he'd wanted her so badly."

"It was disputed by the prosecution. They said that he was too drunk to be able to do anything else.

But I brought in the girl he spent the night with. She testified that he hadn't been too drunk." He shook his head. "It didn't matter. That boy was going to prison no matter what he or I said."

"Why do you think one of the appeals courts didn't reopen the investigation? Why didn't they see any prejudice against him?"

"I don't want to sound like I'm bad-mouthing your father or anyone else, Sheriff," he answered truthfully. "But there was a present state senator involved with this case. And a judge, who's now a city councilman. This man didn't have a chance."

Sharyn thought over his words. "Are you saying that they actively took a role in preventing him from getting a fair appeal?"

He shook his head. "I'm not making any accusations. I can't prove anything. I'm just telling you that there was a drive to put him in jail and a push to keep him there." He frowned and studied the pen he was holding. "I saw that he's going to die later this month. I wish there was something I could do to help him."

"I'm reopening the Bentley case," Sharyn told him. "I think there's a connection between that case and the new murder. I don't think Ronnie Smith killed Leila Bentley."

He looked surprised. "Any suspects?"

"Not really," she admitted ruefully. "Not yet."

"You haven't made this public knowledge then, I take it?"

"No, not yet."

"Take my advice, Sheriff. Make sure you have something concrete going for you, or the press and the people are going to crucify you. Nobody likes to dredge up stuff that causes them to be uncomfortable."

"I know." She sighed, looking at his expensive office.

"I admire you for looking at it though," he told her honestly. "I don't give you much of a chance of doing anything that will save Ronnie Smith's life, but I think you're pretty brave to try, being an elected official and all."

"Thanks," she answered, feeling a little more isolated.

"I got together everything that I have about the case," he told her. "All my notes and my investigations. You're welcome to them."

Sharyn looked up at him, taking in his expensive suit and carefully created hairstyle. "Maybe you could do something as well, Mr. Dakin. Maybe you could get involved with helping me persuade the state that they should wait to execute him until the investigation is over."

Mike Dakin fiddled with his pen again. "That would mean your coming out to the press with your investigation," he said carefully. "It would mean making yourself look bad if you couldn't prove your theory."

"If that's what it takes," she responded lightly. "Will you help?"

"Yes," he agreed when she thought he would probably put her off. "I would like to help. I don't stand to lose anything by making a few calls. You're going to be the big loser here, Sheriff, once you announce the investigation. You better have a flack jacket to protect yourself from debris."

She stood up and smiled securely. "I think I can handle it, Mr. Dakin."

"Good." He stood and shook her hand. "I'll make those calls. My secretary has that information for you on your way out. Good luck, Sheriff. It was nice meeting you."

"You, too, Mr. Dakin," she answered. "Maybe we can pull this off."

She answered the phone in the car as she drove to the office. It was Ernie, breathlessly asking her when she would be arriving at the station.

"Five minutes," she told him. "What's up?"

"Reporters are everywhere, Sheriff," he explained. "We found some new evidence. Joe and Ed picked up David Mauney, the custodian, for questioning."

Chapter Six

There were too many press vans and reporters to park close to the station. Sharyn pulled around the back, but the rear entrance was blocked as well. She got on the phone with Ernie. A few minutes later, Ernie and Ed had cleared the back entrance. Sharyn slipped through, and they locked the gate behind her.

"Is he the right man, Sheriff?" one reporter yelled over the fence.

"Did you find him or did he turn himself in?" another reporter questioned.

Sharyn grimly turned away and walked into the station. "What happened?"

Ernie glanced at Ed and Joe. Sharyn walked into her office, and Ed closed the door behind them.

"Ed and Joe found new evidence when they went

to the school to question a teacher," Ernie told her plainly, his wispy tufts of hair a little more skewed than usual.

"How?" Sharyn wondered, taking off her jacket and hanging it up on the rack.

"It wasn't a search," Ed explained.

"Of course not," she obliged. "You didn't have a warrant."

"We followed David Mauney into the toolshed in the back of the school," Joe continued. "We were looking for the football coach. We thought Mauney could tell us where he was."

Ed nodded. "We walked in behind him, and the hatchet was sitting on a shelf. Right out in the open."

"We sent it to the lab," Ernie advised her.

Sharyn tapped a pencil on her desk. "That borders on illegal search."

"But we weren't searching," Joe reiterated. "It was just there with blood on it."

"What did Mr. Mauney say?" she wondered.

Ed shrugged. "Said he killed a squirrel with it."

"Okay. Let's try to salvage this, huh? Ernie get on the phone and get the DA over here. We need a search warrant to go any farther into that building."

"What about us?"

"Go over and pick up Mrs. Mauney. She was his alibi for that night. Let's see what she has to say."

They nodded, looking relieved, and left the office.

"This could be what you were looking for, Sheriff," Ernie reminded her quietly.

She took a deep breath. She wouldn't have pegged Mr. Mauney for being a violent man. Antisocial, maybe. But not a murderer.

"How did the reporters find out about this?" she asked. Somehow they had managed to have knowledge that should have been restricted. They had knowledge before she did. "Could there be a leak in the office?"

Ernie sighed heavily. "Ed and I were talking about the same thing, Sheriff. How else could those vultures have heard about this? They were here at the same time as the boys were bringing in Mauney."

She shook her head. "I'd hate to think that anyone in this office would have given it away. They all know how important it is to us. It's possible they could have called from the school when Ed and Joe picked him up."

He nodded. "That's possible. He gave them a run for their money. Ed called the shrink in from the hospital to talk to him."

"They didn't hurt him, though, did they?"

Ernie shook his head. "Nah. He had to be restrained, but he's fine."

There was a loud commotion from the main office area. People were shouting. David Matthews yelled back. A shot was fired, then another echoed through the building. Sharyn and Ernie drew their weapons and stayed low as they ran out of her office.

"What happened?" she asked David, who was wrestling someone to the floor.

"Idiot!" he hissed. He pulled Tim Stryker up by the arms after cuffing his hands together. "Little fool!"

"Where is he?" Tim demanded. "He murdered Carrie! I want him dead!"

"Calm down!" Sharyn advised the boy. "You're in trouble now, too."

"I don't care," he shouted. "I want him dead!"

David looked up at her for a decision. The boy had discharged a firearm in the sheriff's office. They couldn't just look the other way, even though they all understood that he was under terrible emotional distress.

"Lock him up," Sharyn said finally. "Let him cool down, and we'll see what we can do."

The press swarmed into the building at the sound of gunfire from inside. Cameras were flashing, and video recorders were scanning the room, finally landing on Tim's distraught face.

"It sure didn't take him long to find out," Ernie concluded as David led the boy away.

"Maybe whoever tipped the press tipped him as well," Sharyn suggested. She glanced around at the pack of reporters and onlookers filling the office.

"Let's get them out of here before anything else stupid happens. This is like a circus."

Trudy's pale face and slightly trembling lip made Sharyn stop and think as she escorted the press from the building. The woman might have just been upset about the whole ugly scene. Or she might have inadvertently leaked some information that had brought the press down on their heads.

David came back after locking Tim up and helped get the office back to normal. Sharyn called Trudy into her office, supposedly for any messages she might have for her. When the door had closed behind her, Trudy broke down, sobbing.

"Oh, Sheriff, I'm so sorry. I didn't know all this would happen," she confessed, her nose turning bright red as she cried.

"What did you do, Trudy?" Sharyn asked, not believing that the woman would have done anything of that sort on purpose. It had to be an accident.

"I spoke to Senator Talbot yesterday," she said, wringing her hands together. "He told me that this case was very important to him because he was from Diamond Springs and because he represents our district. He asked me to keep him informed if there were any changes." She looked up at Sharyn. "I had no idea he would tell the press, Sheriff. You have to believe me. I thought he wanted to know for personal reasons. Just that he'd be so glad that we found the murderer."

Sharyn looked down at her desk calendar. She didn't blame Trudy, although in the future she'd have to make it clearer that she meant not to discuss the case with *anyone,* senator or not. She couldn't believe Caison would go to those lengths either. If he had called and casually asked her what was happening in the case, she probably would have told him. It was an underhanded strategy to make him look better for the press. It had just been dumb luck on Caison's part that something had broken in the case, and Trudy had called him out of a sense of duty.

Trudy stood up on shaky legs. "I'll have my resignation on your desk in fifteen minutes," she told Sharyn softly. "I apologize, Sheriff. I can't imagine what the senator was thinking."

"Trudy," Sharyn started with a smile. "I don't want to lose you over this. There was no way for you to know that Senator Talbot would call the press. Let's just say in the future that we won't give out any information to anyone."

Trudy smiled a watery smile. "I won't even tell my minister if he calls," she promised. "Thank you."

The phone rang, and Nick's voice came through on the line. "Is it true?"

"I'll just leave your messages," Trudy told her when she saw that Sharyn had a call. "Thanks again."

Sharyn smiled. "That's okay. Thanks for the messages."

When the woman left the room, Sharyn picked up the receiver again. "Don't tell me—you saw it on television?"

"Heard it on the radio," he corrected. "Has someone confessed to the crime?"

"No," she admitted. "They picked him up for questioning."

There was a silence on the line, then Nick's voice came through like a shock. "I don't believe it."

"He had opportunity, and they found a weapon."

"What about motive?" he responded impatiently. "Cut the cute stuff."

Sharyn opened a letter with her opener. "I haven't even talked to him yet, Nick. I just got back to the office."

"What are you waiting for?"

"I'm going to talk to him as soon as I get off the phone," she said. "Anything on those gloves?"

"I've narrowed it down to three places in town that sell the gloves," he told her briskly. "Are you losing your backbone on this case?"

She bristled at once. "I'm doing my job." She hung up the receiver and glared at it for a moment. The man was a thorn in her side.

Ernie knocked on the door. "You ready to talk to Mauney?" he wondered.

She nodded. "I'm ready."

"The wife's here, too. What did you say to Trudy?" Ernie whispered as they walked to the interrogation room.

"She told me that she was the one who accidentally let the whole thing out to the press," she explained briefly.

Ernie nodded without looking at the other woman as they passed. "Did you fire her?"

"No," Sharyn replied. "It wasn't her fault. I'll explain later."

Ed and Joe met her at the door. "We figured we should all be in there," Ed told her. "It wouldn't hurt to be extra careful. The man went berserk when we tried to bring him in for questioning."

"You're right," she agreed. "Ernie, you take notes. Ed. Joe." The two men stepped forward, their faces hard with grim determination. "You look menacing."

They both frowned but didn't remark on her words. Ed opened the door, leading the way in before her.

David Mauney was such a nondescript individual that anyone would be hard pressed to make him stand out in a crowd. Everything about him was faded brown, from his eyes and hair to his clothes and boots. He looked from person to person as the sheriff and the three deputies entered the room. Then he studied the tabletop. His hands were clenched fists in front of him.

"Mr. Mauney," Sharyn began, watching him carefully. She put all the preconceived notions out of her head and concentrated on the man. If it turned out to be that this man did kill Carrie Sommers, then Ernie was right. Mauney had been at the school long enough that he could have murdered Leila Bentley as well. "We've talked before. I'm Sheriff Howard."

He looked up at her. "I know who you are." His voice was slightly nasal, as though he were just getting over a cold.

"Would you like to tell me and my deputies about what happened Saturday morning?"

"I already told you. All of you." He glared at each of them. Ed pulled away from the wall he'd been leaning against but didn't say anything.

"We'd like to hear it again, Mr. Mauney," she told him. "Just take your time."

He fidgeted in his chair. "All right. I was fishing at the lake until after the prom was over. Then I went up and did my job and went home. Enough?"

Ed came to stand behind his chair. "What time was that?"

"What difference does it make?"

Sharyn interceded. "You have to know that you're in trouble here, Mr. Mauney. We just need a few answers."

"It was four A.M. when I got home. I didn't see any dead girl. I didn't see her car. I don't go around to that side of the parking lot."

"Did you see anyone else?" Ed demanded.

"No one. Only an old fool like me who's got nothing would be doing that kind of job for the money I make."

"What about the hatchet with the blood on it?" Sharyn asked calmly.

"It's squirrel blood," Mauney told her. "I killed a squirrel for supper."

"You know we can tell if you're lying," Ed said in a menacing voice.

The man was up off his chair in an instant. He roared about being called a liar and went for Ed's throat. It took both deputies to subdue him.

"I think we should let the shrink talk to him," Ernie said slowly.

Sharyn agreed. "Let's talk to his wife."

"Leave her out of this," Mauney yelled, thrashing in the chair again.

"We'll be back, Mr. Mauney," Sharyn promised him. "Try to calm down."

Ernie and Sharyn left the interrogation room together. Trudy hailed them and pointed to a young girl seated in a chair near the door.

"She says she has information for you, Sheriff. About this case."

"I'll talk to her first," Sharyn told Ernie. "You get on the phone and find out what's keeping that DA."

The girl's name was LeAnn Hart. She was a graduating senior, and she knew Carrie Sommers. They weren't best friends, but they "hung out" occasionally.

Sharyn showed the girl into her office, then closed the door and took her place behind the desk. She noticed LeAnn glancing up at the fierce picture of her grandfather. The girl shuddered delicately.

"Okay, LeAnn. What do you have to tell me?"

"It's about Mr. Mauney. A lot of us think that he does something to the cars."

"Something like what?"

The girl shrugged. "I don't know. But I drive a new car, and it's broken down twice at school. My mechanic looked at it and said there was nothing wrong. But it broke down again, and Mr. Mauney fixed it."

Sharyn nearly yawned. "Maybe Mr. Mauney is a better mechanic."

"The same thing has happened to other girls at school. It happened to Carrie. I think that might be why she couldn't leave the prom right away."

Sharyn thought about the unlatched hood on Carrie's car. "How many other girls has it happened to?"

"Ten or so that I know about," LeAnn answered. "All cheerleaders. Always blond." She tossed back her own blond hair with a casual hand.

Sharyn studied her, thinking about her words. There but for the grace of God, LeAnn might have been Carrie that night after the prom. The case seemed to be closing in around David Mauney.

"Is there anything else?" Sharyn asked.

"That's it," LeAnn told her.

"Are there any other girls who can corroborate your story?"

"What?"

"Anyone else with the same story," Sharyn explained.

"Oh, sure." She giggled. "I guess that's cop slang, huh?"

"Yeah," Sharyn agreed. She stood up. "Thanks for stopping by, LeAnn."

"No prob. I just want to help Carrie. I just got back from the beach and heard about it. I think Mr. Mauney killed her."

"I don't know yet," Sharyn told her. "But we'll be in touch."

"Well?" Ernie asked as she escorted the girl from her office.

Sharyn told him what the girl told her. "It would explain the hood being left open on Carrie's car."

Ernie snorted. "The man's some kind of pervert at the very least."

"She didn't say he was looking up their dresses," Sharyn reminded him. "Let's talk to the wife."

Susan Mauney was waiting for them. "Have you arrested my husband?"

"Not yet, Mrs. Mauney," Ernie told her. "Maybe we could sit down and talk about all of this."

The woman nodded and took a seat, folding her arms in front of her on the table. "What can I tell you? David's not a murderer."

"What time does your husband usually get home, Mrs. Mauney?" Sharyn asked.

The other woman shook her graying head. She was as gray and colorless as her husband. "Probably between six and six-thirty. Unless there's a special event."

"What about after the prom last week?"

"He was home by four A.M. I woke up when he came in and asked him if he wanted something to eat. He told me that he'd already had a sandwich while he was fishing and didn't want anything else."

"Mrs. Mauney, did you know your husband has been tampering with the girls' cars at school?"

Susan Mauney frowned. "It wouldn't surprise me, I guess. He likes attention. He does things like that to get attention sometimes."

"Things like what?" Ernie wondered.

She shrugged. "One time, I knew the can opener wasn't broken, but he says he fixed it. Once he told the neighbor that he fixed a place in his fence that was broken when it wasn't."

"Why do you think he does these things?" Sharyn asked quietly.

"To feel important, to feel special. We all need

to feel special, don't we, Sheriff? David has shrapnel in his leg that is very painful to him. Some
nights he can't sleep for walking around to keep it
from hurting him. He thought when he came home
from the army that he was going to be a hero. He
wasn't. He never got over it."

"So, you're saying that he does something to
keep the girls' cars from starting for attention,"
Sharyn repeated. "Why the pretty blond girls?"

Susan Mauney drew an old photo from her purse.
The picture was of a good-looking man in a uniform
and a pretty young blonde. "That's us in our senior
year at Diamond Springs High School, Sheriff. I'm
not a doctor, but maybe he's pretending he's doing
it for me. I was pretty then, wasn't I?"

Sharyn nodded, then passed the picture to Ernie.
"Can I keep this for a while, Mrs. Mauney?"

"Anything to help my husband," she declared.
"We don't have much money, but—"

"If your husband is arrested, the state will provide
an attorney for him," Ernie told her.

Sharyn smiled at the woman and thought about
Mike Dakin. Would David Mauney be railroaded
the same way, whether he was guilty or not?

"You can go home now, Mrs. Mauney. We'll call
you if anything else changes."

"What about my husband?"

"He'll have to stay, at least for the time being,"
Sharyn explained. "We'll try to get through all of

this as soon as we can. Ernie will take you home. Thanks for coming in."

Ernie glanced at Sharyn. "Don't you need me here?"

"I'll fill you in when you get back. Good-bye, Mrs. Mauney."

"Good-bye, Sheriff. If it makes any difference, I voted for you last election."

"Thanks, Mrs. Mauney." Sharyn sighed. "I wish it was that simple."

Sharyn watched them leave the station. The whole thing just didn't feel right to her. Maybe Mauney was guilty. His wife's statement wouldn't mean much in court. He couldn't prove he didn't murder Carrie, then go home. The time frame wasn't that tight. The Mauneys lived barely a mile from the school. It was possible. They needed more information.

She found Ed in her office. "The doc's with Mauney. Joe stayed in there with him."

"Where's David?"

"Out on patrol. We were both afraid things might get hairy tonight. The town's on edge."

She smiled blandly. "Like the time after Leila died, huh?"

He nodded, giving in to the similarities. "A lot of things change, but a lot of things stay the same."

"I know."

"What can I do?" he asked finally, disturbing her reverie.

"I need you to go down to the impound and have someone take a look at Carrie's car. I need to know if there was something wrong and what it was."

"Are we trying to prove he killed Leila, too?" Ed asked her.

Sharyn faced him. "We're trying to find the killer. However that goes. Whoever that is. Okay?"

He nodded and left her office. Sharyn sank back in her chair and closed her eyes.

In some ways, it would be easy to believe David Mauney was guilty. The man was strange. He didn't fit into the community. People would buy him as a murderer, even in Leila's case. But was he really guilty of anything besides being moody and keeping to himself?

She checked her Rolodex and dialed Nick's number.

"What?"

"Sorry to bother you."

"Oh, it's you. The press has been going crazy. I've had to restrict the morgue to only a few people."

"Mauney's with the shrink. I spoke with his wife and a girl from the school who claims he tampered with their cars so that he could repair them."

"But you aren't convinced?"

"About the cars? It seems to fit the open hood on

Carrie's car. They're taking a look at the engine in the impound."

"What does his wife say?"

"She says it's possible. She says he likes attention," she informed him blandly.

"I think he's an ornery man with a chip on his shoulder. But that doesn't make him a murderer. I think if he wanted to murder someone, he wouldn't have left her looking so pretty and sweet. It would have been messy and ugly."

"Are you willing to stake your reputation on it?"

"That doesn't matter, does it?" he asked. "Are you willing to stake *your* reputation on my findings?"

Sharyn shook her head tiredly. "I don't know. When the DA hears everything, there's going to be a push to indict him."

"What can I do? I know you didn't call for my opinion."

She grinned. That was Nick. "I wanted you to look over those old files and see if you find any reference to Leila Bentley's car being tampered with."

"You could be signing Mauney's death certificate if there is."

"I know," she admitted to him. "But feelings aside, there could be a lot of hard evidence here."

"If they indict this man for killing Carrie Sommers, they'll have the wrong man again, Sharyn."

"Neither one of us knows that until some of the lab work comes back."

The line went dead in her hand, and she put down the receiver. She was going to have to stop thinking that way. If they found the girl's blood on that hatchet and both girls' cars had been tampered with, she was going to believe that David Mauney was guilty of killing Carrie Sommers. End of story.

"Sheriff." Trudy knocked on the door, then stuck her head around the corner. "Charlie Sommers is here with a bail bondsman and a lawyer to get Tim Stryker out of jail."

Sharyn sighed heavily as she stood up from her desk. Was the day ever going to be over?

Chapter Seven

Charlie Sommers greeted her coldly. "I can't believe you're going to charge that boy with attempted murder."

"I haven't charged him with anything yet," she informed him tautly. "When I do, his parents will be the first to know."

"They're out of town," Charlie told her. "I'm going to get him out of here. I was hoping my lawyer here might be able to get you to listen to reason."

The lawyer smiled and advanced towards Sharyn, with his hand outstretched to take her own. "Percy. Eldeon Percy."

"Sharyn Howard." She shook his hand. "Tim Stryker hasn't been charged with anything yet. We're holding him for his own protection. He discharged a firearm in this office. He might pose a threat to himself or to someone else."

"Perhaps he could be released into my client's custody?" Eldeon Percy suggested.

Sharyn shook her head. "He's a minor. Mr. Sommers isn't the boy's legal guardian; I can only release Tim into his parents' custody. Unless Mr. Sommers has written consent from the Strykers to take on this obligation."

The lawyer looked at Charlie Sommers, who shook his head and glared at Sharyn.

"If not, then we'll have to keep him until we feel he isn't a threat, we charge him or his parents come back. Sorry Mr. Percy. Mr. Sommers."

"It's true though, isn't it?" Charlie Sommers stared as though he could see through the walls to where they were holding David Mauney. "That snake that killed my daughter is here."

"We have a man in custody whom we're questioning about the incident," she admitted carefully. "We're trying to discover the truth."

"He killed Carrie! What else do you need to know?"

Sharyn decided that enough was enough. "I think you should go home, Mr. Sommers. As soon as we know anything that's certain, we'll get back with you."

"Don't you want him to be guilty, Sheriff?" He

asked her harshly. "Is there someone else you'd rather see take the blame for it?"

She looked at him steadily. "I think you should take your client home now, Mr. Percy. Before he spends the night in jail for his own safety as well."

"I think you should do your job, Sheriff," Charlie Sommers replied. "All these years that man's been working at the school, waiting for the right time."

"I think we should leave, Charlie." Eldeon Percy tried to persuade him. "This is over the line."

"My daughter is dead," the other man answered. "That's what's over the line. They couldn't protect my baby."

The District Attorney arrived at that moment with a flurry of camera flashes and questions yelled out on the frosty air. He was accompanied by Senator Talbot, who turned to face the press before he entered the long, low building that was the sheriff's office.

"We've come to answer your questions," Senator Talbot boomed over the sound of voices and the blinding flashes. "District Attorney Michaelson and I have come to right this terrible wrong."

"That's right," the DA yelled, not as convincingly as the senator, who'd had years to perfect his talent at crowd pleasing. "I'm here to indict David Mauney on the charge of first-degree murder in the death of Carrie Sommers."

The crowd outside the station became frenzied.

Ernie came through the back door at the same time that Joe came out of the interrogation room. The dispatcher called David back to the station.

"Should we call the highway patrol?" Ernie wondered, thinking that there were too many of them for the small group in the station to subdue.

Charlie Sommers stood outside with the senator, inflaming the people who were waiting to hear something about the case.

"We'll be fine," Sharyn told him. "Just stay here."

She walked outside into the freezing air. The crowd saw her and started yelling again. She didn't wait for Caison or the DA to make room for her. The press had set up a speaking area, raised slightly, and a microphone to address the crowd. The senator had thought of everything.

Cameras flashed, blinding her, and video cameras zoomed in on her face.

"I'm Sheriff Sharyn Howard," she said to the crowd, adjusting the microphone to suit her needs. "I think I know most of you."

People yelled her name and shouted questions that were indistinguishable in the mass of voices speaking at once.

"I know all of you are looking for an answer to this terrible crime. So are we." She paused and looked out into the crowd as they began to fall silent to hear her words. "But we can't find it like this.

Mr. Sommers is hurt and wants to hurt someone in return for his daughter's death. I don't think any of us can blame him for that. But I don't think any of us want him running through town shooting people either. That's why you elected me. My deputies and I are looking for the truth in all of this. You have to give us the opportunity to find it. So if you don't have police business to take care of here, I want you to go home, and when we know something about Carrie's death, I promise you that I will make a statement."

"What about the man you've got right now, Sheriff?" a reporter asked.

"We do have a man here while we check out his story. I'm sure any of you with family would want us to do the same for your family member. Nothing else is going to happen out here today. So I'd like you to clear the area. Go home and take some time with your own children today, for Carrie's sake. Her funeral is the day after tomorrow. We need to show her how much we really care by our actions."

Charlie Sommers was weeping openly and leaning heavily on his lawyer's arm.

"You promise us that you'll let us know when anything happens?" the nearest television reporter demanded.

"You have my word," she replied.

The press didn't leave the area, but they did move back to a respectable distance away from the front door. The people who had flocked to the office just to get a glimpse of the killer began to move away, talking among themselves and helping Charlie Sommers back to his car.

Senator Talbot glared at her. "You diffused that quite nicely, Sheriff. But you can't make the DA go away."

"We aren't ready to present," she addressed the lawyer.

He looked baffled. "I thought—" He looked at the senator. "I thought you were ready to present your case against this man and file charges."

"The investigation is still ongoing. Right now all we have is opportunity and a hatchet that might have squirrel blood on it. We need the lab work in, or we're going to look like fools."

"But he didn't have an alibi," Caison reminded her.

"Yes, he did, but his facts didn't all add up. I still have reason to doubt that he committed this murder."

"What?" the DA pondered. "You said yourself that you have opportunity."

"I think he has a few problems," she told him. "He's talking to a psychiatrist from the hospital. That doesn't make him a killer."

The DA physically balked at that. "Senator, we'll have to wait to make another move until the investigation has progressed." After all, he was up for reelection as well. This case could be a feather in his cap. Or an anchor around his neck.

The senator stared him down. "I want to move on this now."

"I can't. If I move now and the case is bad, or the man has a mental problem, I'll look like an idiot." He looked at Sharyn. "You'll call me when you finish up?"

She nodded. "Before I call the press."

Sharyn was left standing on the cold doorstep with the angry senator. The wind whipped both of their clothes and hair. The crowd was gone, but the media was still camped out on the dead grass. A few of them looked their way but decided there was no story to tell from their meeting.

"Well, I suppose I might as well go, Sheriff."

"I suppose you might as well," she agreed blandly.

"Don't even think of cutting short this investigation and letting this man go because you feel sorry for him. Or because you've got cold feet about proving this case."

Sharyn smiled and looked out at the street. "I'll investigate this case until we know the truth, Senator. If that means that this man is guilty, I'll be glad to put him away. If not, I'll do what I have to do."

Caison Talbot caught her eye. "Don't press me, girl. You don't want to be on my bad side."

She didn't look away. "Is this your good side, Senator?"

He chuckled as though it didn't mean anything to him, but Sharyn knew he was irritated. "I don't think you want to fight me, Sheriff."

"You're right," she agreed. "Why does this mean so much to you? You've done so much for this area while you've been in office. Surely you aren't worried about what people are going to think?"

His gaze was wintry. "Leave it alone, Sheriff. Just do your job if you want to keep it."

He walked away. The reporters ignored his leaving. Sharyn shook her head, wishing she could make some sense of it all. The case was ten years old. What difference did it make to him if she discovered that they had arrested the wrong man? As she'd found with her own mother, pride and sentiment went deep.

A burst of applause greeted her as she walked back into the station. She smiled and waved them away. "If you can still do that when this is all over, and we still have our jobs, we'll go party."

Sharyn closed herself in her office while Ernie went to harass the lab people to work faster. Ed was still with the impound mechanics. Joe and the doctor were still locked up with Mauney. She put in a call to George Albert, intending to get to the bottom of the senator's fears about the case. He called her

back about a half an hour later during a break between sessions.

"I caught you on television," he greeted her.
"You looked convincing."

"Thanks," she replied. "It worked anyway. For
now. I have a question for you, sir. Why does this
whole Leila Bentley case mean so much to the
senator?"

"I was wondering that myself," he answered. "I
think I may have found the answer."

"I'd be interested in hearing it."

"It seems the governor has selected a panel to go
back and check out all of the senator's cases from
when he was a prosecuting attorney. There's been
some question of ethics."

"Ethics?"

"There might be a class action lawsuit raised
against Senator Talbot. Your case could add fuel to
that controversy, and the publicity alone could hurt
him."

"What about you, George?" she wondered.
"Aren't you worried about the case?"

He laughed. "There were plenty of trials that Caison and I worked on together. But I'm not worried
about being hanged with him, if that's what you
mean. I've done enough work of my own without
him that I can stand on. Besides, Sharyn, I wasn't
involved with any underhanded dealings. If Caison

was, and I'm not saying that he was, mind you, then he'll have to answer to it."

"Well, that makes sense anyway," she responded. "More sense than him worrying about not being re-elected because of a single mistake ten years ago."

"Watch your step, Sharyn; Caison is a powerful enemy."

"I can imagine. Thanks, George."

"Why don't you come for dinner tonight? Richard's looking forward to seeing you again. He's a changed man, Sharyn."

"George, is Richard going out on his own?"

"Not yet," he returned. "We wanted him to have a chance to get acclimated again. Not that he's acted like he wants to go out. He's been content just being home with his mother. Of course, who wouldn't be?"

"I'll be there," she said.

Ed burst into her office. "We just finished looking at the car again, Sheriff. The girl was right. The car wouldn't have started."

"Why not?"

"Somebody removed the ignition coil wire."

Sharyn considered his words. It was like a death knell for any chance that David Mauney wouldn't be indicted. She couldn't shield him forever.

"You don't look so happy," he observed. "I thought this would put your theory one step closer to being real."

He was right, of course. But she wasn't satisfied. She looked up at him. "I'm still waiting for all of the information to come in."

"Maybe you were right, Sheriff. The two murders might have been committed by the same person."

"I know." *But not David Mauney.*

"I'm heading for home now," he said. "Call me if you need me."

"Thanks, Ed. Good work."

When he had gone, she started back through the pile of paperwork that had quickly accumulated on her desk. Some of it was information from the Bentley case.

Nick called and told her that either they didn't think to check the car to see if it would start, or they didn't have that problem. Either way, the information couldn't be matched to the case. If the hood of the car had been unlatched on Leila's car, there was no notation of it. Sharyn believed her father would have noticed it if the car hadn't started or the hood was left open, even in their haste to find a suspect. She didn't believe that he had mishandled the original case so much as that he didn't have the second case to compare it to.

But then maybe Mauney was guilty of Carrie's murder but not Leila's. Maybe the two cases weren't connected, despite her strong feelings to the contrary.

Joe knocked on the door. "Sheriff, we're finished. This is the shrink from the hospital."

"Come in, Doctor." Sharyn greeted him and shook her head when Joe asked silently if she wanted him to stay. "I'm Sheriff Howard."

"The lady sheriff." The younger man nodded as he took her hand. "I'm Josh Hartsell."

"So what's the verdict?" she asked at once.

Dr. Hartsell took a seat and shook his head. "The man has some problems, Sheriff. I won't kid you on that. He's paranoid and depressed. He relives the Vietnam war with way too much frequency. I'm not sure that sometimes it couldn't verge on complete separation with reality."

"So you're saying he could have killed that girl?"

He laughed. "I wish it was that simple, Sheriff. We're all *capable* of killing. Mr. Mauney is certainly capable of killing. But I don't think he's capable of killing in this case. I read the reports, looked at the pictures. I just don't see him as some kind of gentleman killer."

"Meaning he wouldn't have been so neat?'

"Meaning if he was delusional, he probably would have cut the girl in half."

Sharyn sat back in her chair. "Then who are we looking for, Doctor Hartsell? Do you have some profile of this person you could give me after reading the facts?"

He shrugged. "I think the killer is basically a

careful person. He or she was very detached from the victim. It's even possible that he or she saw the victim as being like a doll of some kind: The painstaking attempt to keep it clean and neat, not to mess up the body, leaving her looking pretty and untouched. This is clearly a personality that views itself and others from a distance."

"So you don't think this was a statement of some kind?"

"Not really. I'd say it was more like a compulsion. In fact, it wouldn't surprise me to find that this person is obsessive-compulsive. These girls probably represent someone in his or her own life, maybe someone he or she blames for a problem."

Sharyn nodded. "Thanks for your help, Doctor Hartsell. If you could write all of that into a report and fax it to us, I'd really appreciate it."

"Thanks, Sheriff. It was nice to meet you. By the way, I voted for you."

"Thanks."

Sharyn yawned and stretched and looked at the time. It was nearly six-thirty. "Has the prisoner had dinner?" she asked Trudy.

"Which one?" Trudy wondered, holding two trays.

Sharyn snapped her fingers. In all the commotion, she'd forgotten about Tim Stryker. "I'll take this in to him," she said. "Have Joe take a tray into Mauney."

Trudy nodded. "I'm on overtime in five minutes."

"Have Joe take a tray, then get out of here," Sharyn replied. "I'll see you tomorrow."

Sharyn opened the door to the holding area where they were keeping Tim. He sat with his head in his hands, staring at the floor without moving.

"Hungry?" she asked, startling him.

"No. I couldn't eat."

She put the tray down on the table. "Better keep up your strength. You'll need it at the prison when you get there."

He eyed her warily. "I've ruined my whole life."

Sharyn looked back at him. "Not yet."

He shook his head. "I'm going to go to prison. I have a scholarship for UNC Wilmington this fall to study marine biology."

She sat down on the bunk across from him. "What you did was wrong and stupid. No one can excuse you from that. We can decide that you were overwrought because of Carrie's death, and we can ask the judge for leniency. Your parents are on their way home. Between us, we can work this out."

"Really?" he asked, sniffing and wiping his eyes with the back of his hand.

"If you give me your word that you won't let something stupid like this happen again. You know Carrie wouldn't have wanted you to screw up your whole life to avenge her."

"I know," he whispered. "I don't know what I was thinking."

"We'll assume you weren't," she finished, getting to her feet. "And we'll go from there."

Tim smiled a little. "Thanks, Sheriff."

"Don't thank me yet. There's bound to be some community service in this for you. It's not going to be easy to get through this."

"Carrie's funeral is tomorrow," he said. "Will my parents be able to have me out of here by then?"

"If not, someone from here will take you," she promised. "We'll work that out, too, Tim. Now eat your supper."

Tim Stryker was a good kid, she thought, closing the door behind her. He had a bright future. He just needed to get through this terrible point in his life. And he didn't need any encouragement from people like Charlie Sommers. When his parents came home, she felt sure they could straighten him up.

Could it get more complicated? she wondered, going back to her office. She felt certain that there was something missing. Some piece of the puzzle that they hadn't seen yet. Not that she couldn't move to have the DA indict Mauney on what they had already. She just wanted to be sure.

"Line 2." Ernie buzzed through to her office.

"Sharyn? Sharyn Howard?" A voice came from the other end of the line.

"Yes. Who is this?"

"It's Sandy Huffman," the voice replied. "Remember me?"

As if she could forget her! Sandy had been her only friend in high school before college and other obligations split them apart. "Sandy! How are you?"

"I'm fine, and I'm back in town for the reunion. Maybe we could get together for a drink?"

"That would be great," Sharyn enthused.

"Good. I'm looking forward to hearing about what you decided to do with your life. And I want you to meet my husband and my son. You're going to the anniversary prom, aren't you?"

Sharyn rolled her eyes toward the ceiling. "If I can get away."

"It doesn't come around every day," Sandy reminded her. "I'll see you later."

Sandy Huffman. They had seen each other for the last time at graduation. She had hated the fact that even dead, Leila Bentley got more attention than they did at the ceremony. Sandy and Sharyn had been friends through high school, probably because they were always together alphabetically.

So Sandy was married and had a son, Sharyn mused. They had both sworn that they weren't going to get married since neither girl had a date all through high school. Sandy had always said that the boys were too afraid of Sharyn's father to ask her out for a date. She never had an adequate reason why she wasn't asked out.

But now she was married and had a family. Sharyn looked at her grandfather's picture and wondered where he had found time for a family. Of course, it would be a little different for her; he didn't have to go through pregnancy and childbirth.

The phone rang and Sharyn answered it. "Sheriff Howard? This is Mike Dakin. I just wanted to let you know that the state is going through with Ronnie Smith's execution on schedule."

"There was nothing you could do to delay it?"

"Not with the news about you arresting another man for the Sommers murder. What's the point?"

"I don't think the man in custody murdered Carrie. But if he did, there's still every possibility that he killed Leila as well."

"Well, the state has to have more than just your theory, Sheriff."

"It's become a circus here. The media is moving faster than we are."

"Welcome to the real world, Sheriff! Are you prepared to accuse this man of killing Leila Bentley?"

Sharyn hesitated. Was she prepared to implicate Mauney for Leila's murder when she wasn't sure about Carrie's?

"Well, there's nothing I can do about the execution," he continued after she didn't respond. It's set for the day after tomorrow at one A.M. Without more evidence or some sign that the case has been seriously reopened, they won't move on it."

Sharyn looked at the phone in her hand. "Thanks for calling, Mr. Dakin. I'll take care of it."

Chapter Eight

Sharyn tapped the microphone in the early morning air. It was freezing. The sky was a clear, bright blue. She thought that her face was probably the same shade. She had stood outside the office for about a half an hour waiting for the press to assemble.

She had considered her next course of action all through the long, sleepless night. It seemed to her that there was no other way. The state had to be convinced of her sincerity in the case.

"We are going to be reopening another murder case that we believe is linked to this one."

"Was there another murder?" a reporter demanded.

"Ten years ago," Sharyn explained, feeling panic in her stomach like a clenched fist. "Leila Bentley

134

was murdered in the same parking lot in much the same way. I believe that both of these murders may have been committed by the same person."

The media was buzzing. "Hasn't there been an arrest in that case, Sheriff?"

"In fact, there was an arrest in that case ten years ago. Ronald James Smith has been serving time in state prison for the death of Leila Bentley. It is our contention that he did not commit this crime. We are investigating the theory that both murders are the work of the same person."

"David Mauney?" someone yelled out to her.

She didn't reply.

"Sheriff! Sheriff!" Reporters vied with one another to get her attention.

"One more question," she allowed, feeling her feet going numb in the cold.

"Sheriff, isn't it true that your own father was the arresting officer on that case? Are you saying that he botched the job?"

"My father was in charge of that case," she admitted slowly. "As soon as we know more, we'll let you know. Thank you."

Ernie stood beside the switchboard operator. Both of their faces were a comic study in shock and uncertainty. "I hope you know what you're doing," he managed to say in a hoarse voice.

"I hope so, too," she replied evenly. She went into her office and closed the door behind her.

Trudy brought her coffee at eight-thirty and told her that Tim Stryker's parents were on their way to the station.

"Have the juvie officer meet us here," she told her, not looking up from the paperwork spread out on her desk. "And send Ernie in."

There was a knock on the door, and she looked up, expecting Ernie. It was Ed and Joe. "Mind if we have a word with you, Sheriff?" Ed asked.

"What's on your minds?"

They glanced at one another. "Joe and I have a problem with this whole investigation. We think you're wrong."

Sharyn picked up a pencil. "Wrong? About the two cases being linked together or about David Mauney?"

"No, we agree that Mauney probably did it," Ed said quickly.

"It's this other thing, Sheriff," Joe filled in. "It was sort of sudden for you to announce to the press that you were reopening the case."

"It was," she agreed. "But I didn't have any choice. It was the only way to get the state to take the investigation seriously enough to hold off Ronnie Smith's execution."

"Is that what this is all about?" Joe wondered. "Saving that worthless tramp's life?"

"We were there, Sheriff," Ed reminded her. "You weren't. You didn't see what a low-life thing he was."

"You're right." She nodded, looking at both men closely. "I wasn't there, but take a look at all of these files. You think that I'm prejudiced in favor of these murders being done by the same man. I think you two are prejudiced against it. You aren't willing to take an honest look at the case without feeling as though you've betrayed the past."

Ed shook his head. "We don't feel that way."

"Then let's investigate the possibility," she persuaded. "If it doesn't exist, then I'll be embarrassed, and we'll move on."

Joe shrugged. "We just don't see it, Sheriff."

"Take a look at everything," she invited, handing the file to him. "Then I want you to go out and talk to whomever we can find who still lives here. Anyone that Leila knew. Anyone who was involved in the first case."

Ed looked at the case file, then at Joe. "I guess you're right, Sheriff. You're the one who's going to catch all of it if you're wrong. But it makes the rest of us look bad, too."

"And what about Mauney?" Joe asked.

Sharyn stood up slowly. "I didn't ask for any of this. I sure didn't want my father's case to be reinvestigated. And believe me, no one could give me a harder time than my mother over all of this. They might not reelect me, but I have to live with her."

Joe laughed and Ed grinned, despite himself.

"As for Mauney, we can't do anything until we hear back from the lab. In the meantime, let's see what else we can find out about all of this."

"Okay, Sheriff. Let's take a look at it."

"Yeah, I was stupid and young back then anyway. How embarrassed could I be about being wrong?" Ed asked, looking at his partner.

Sharyn sat back down and took a deep breath. Another crisis averted. For the time being anyway. They had been swamped with calls all morning, the fallout from her announcement to the press. Mike Dakin had called as well, though, and told her that the state was going to take the petition to hold back Ronnie Smith's execution seriously, at least until the investigation was complete. The state attorney general's office had called as well to let her know that her office would be under investigation because of alleged misdoing that might have ended in an innocent man's execution. If Ronnie Smith was released and had to be compensated for their mistake, somebody was going to pay for it.

Her mother wouldn't speak to her. Her aunt was angry because she wouldn't come for a dress fitting. Was there anything else?

She left the office with Ernie, unusually silent beside her. They were going out to visit Leila Bentley's parents. Sharyn had spoken with them, and they had agreed to be interviewed. It had been ten years, but like everyone else in Diamond Springs, the hurt was still apparent in their voices. It seemed as though Leila's death was going to cause as much controversy now as it had ten years ago.

"There's something missing, Ernie," she said, thinking out loud as she often did with him. "Something that none of us is seeing in all of this. It's right in front of us. All we have to do is see it."

Ernie chose his words carefully. "I've been with you for the past two years, Sheriff. I think this is wishful thinking on your part."

Sharyn was hurt but wouldn't say so. If anyone was going to believe in her, she had expected it to be Ernie. He always supported her. "I don't really see myself as a fanciful person, Ernie. Would you mind telling me why you think I would want something like this to happen?"

"I don't know," he replied tautly. "I think it was something from the beginning that affected you about this case. Maybe it's trying to outdo your daddy. Maybe it's just something strange that's come over you."

"Ernie, I can't tell you to read the evidence in both cases again. I know you gathered most of it. Why doesn't it strike you as being too similar to be coincidental?"

"I don't know," he admitted. "I don't see it the way you do."

"Ernie, the girls were found in the same parking lot. They were both killed on the night of the prom. They were both pretty blondes—"

"I know the evidence," he reminded her pointedly. "You don't need to recite it to me."

Sharyn sighed. "I don't want us to argue, Ernie. You've been my friend as well as my assistant. I need you to help me with this. Can we both agree to suspend judgment until we finish the investigation?"

He nodded, words failing him in the face of her confession. "I'll do the best I can, Sheriff."

"That's all I ask." She smiled at him. "I can't imagine doing this without you."

He smiled back sadly. "You know if you're wrong, after this announcement, they'll run you out of office."

"I know. It's a chance I have to take."

"All right." He gave in. "I'll do the best I can for you, Sheriff."

"Thanks, Ernie."

The Bentleys still lived in the same house where they had raised Leila and her brother. The house was shuttered as though it held its terrible sadness closely. Sharyn recalled hearing that Mrs. Bentley had gone away for a while after her daughter's death. When she had returned, everyone was surprised, and there was talk of a suicide attempt and time spent in a psychiatric ward.

To Sharyn, the Bentley house epitomized the way the town felt about Leila's death. Closed in on itself, sorrow beyond sorrow. Even in the summer, the manicured lawns and pretty flowers seemed to weep for their loss.

"Mrs. Bentley." Sharyn greeted the woman who opened the door. "Mr. Bentley." She acknowledged the man who stood behind her. "I'm sorry to bother you with all of this."

"Come in, Sheriff," Anita Bentley said. "It's been a long time. I remember you from school functions with Leila. You've grown very pretty."

Sharyn was embarrassed by Mrs. Bentley's words and her frank appraisal of her freckled face. She felt her cheeks heat up. "I—uh—thank you, Mrs. Bentley."

"Come in and sit down, Sheriff. Is that you, Ernie Watkins?"

Ernie bobbed his head. "Yes, ma'am. How've you been?"

"We've been good, haven't we, Stuart?" She turned to her husband.

"What's this about, Sheriff?" Mr. Bentley cut to the chase.

Sharyn explained everything to them and asked for their help. "I'm trying to establish a pattern between the two crimes."

"I understand, Sheriff," Anita Bentley replied graciously. "We'll do what we can to help."

"Thanks. I need to ask you a few questions about the last few days before Leila's death."

"All right."

"Do you recall her saying anything about someone following her? Did she notice anything being different at school?"

Anita looked at her husband. "I don't recall her saying anything like that, Sheriff. She was looking forward to the dance. She was very excited about her dress and her plans for the future. She was going to go to college that fall."

"Do you remember anything being wrong with her car? After her death, do you recall what happened to her car?"

"We sold it," Stuart Bentley said quickly.

"Did it run afterward? Was the engine operable?" Sharyn asked.

"I don't really know. No one mentioned it. A company contacted us and took it away from the police impound. We never saw it again after the night that Leila drove it to the prom."

"Had Leila ever mentioned having car trouble?"

Stuart Bentley scoffed, "Of course not! It was a new car!"

Anita Bentley frowned. "Now that you mention it, Sheriff, she did have trouble getting the car started a few times."

"What?" her husband asked. "What are you saying?"

"We didn't think anything of it, Stuart. Some boy at school always got it started for her. It wasn't a big deal."

"Did you have the car checked out to see what was wrong with it?" Sharyn queried.

"Yes, she took it into the shop a few weeks before the prom, but the mechanic said he couldn't find anything wrong with it. He suggested that she might have been flooding the engine when she tried to start it," said Mrs. Bentley.

"I know this is difficult for you both," Sharyn remarked. "I appreciate your help."

"Is that it?" Anita Bentley asked in obvious relief. She looked down at the tissue that she had shredded in her hand.

"That's it," Sharyn assured her, standing. "Thanks."

"Do you really think that the man in prison didn't murder Leila?" Anita Bentley asked her.

Sharyn faced her squarely. "I really think the two murders were committed by one person, Mrs. Bentley. I know that must seem strange to you."

"Not at all," she replied calmly. "I never believed that young man did the crime."

"Anita!" her husband barked.

"It's true." She looked at them all. "It was just a feeling I had." She took out a picture, faded with time but still clear. "I brought this out in case it might help. I took this just before Leila and her boyfriend left for the prom. She was so beautiful."

Sharyn studied the picture. Not that she needed to see it to know that Leila was a beautiful girl. "She was as nice as she was beautiful," she murmured.

"Thank you, Sheriff." Tears glistened on Anita Bentley's eyelashes.

Sharyn and Ernie thanked them again and left the husband and wife still arguing.

"I guess you aren't the only one with that feeling," Ernie commented when they had reached the car.

"Except that she felt that way before I even thought about it," Sharyn answered.

"Well, at least she thinks she did," Ernie replied. "People can be led sometimes, Sheriff."

Sharyn refused to be drawn into an argument about the choice that she had made. "We know that Leila did have some trouble starting her car. It's possible the hood was unlocked on her car as well, and no one picked up on it."

"Or our killer got sloppy with the second murder," Ernie proposed.

"Or that he was interrupted."

They were silent for a long moment while Ernie headed the patrol car back to the station. Sharyn studied the picture Mrs. Bentley had given her.

There was something different about it that bothered her at once, but she couldn't put her finger on it.

"What's so interesting?" he asked as she continued to stare at it.

Sharyn shrugged and put the picture away. "I'm not really sure. There's something there that seems strange."

"You've probably been looking at too many pictures of that girl."

"You're probably right. I'm leaving early tonight to have dinner with George Albert and his wife. That'll take my mind off of it for a while. Maybe it'll come to me then."

"Sounds like a good idea," Ernie approved. "You could use some time off."

Sharyn picked up her car at the station, then headed for home. The DA had called several times for her while she had been gone, but she knew it could wait until the next day. She didn't have anything more to tell him. He probably thought since she had announced that she was reopening the Bentley case that she was ready to charge David Mauney. Nothing could be further from the truth.

Even though similarities seemed to exist between the murders, she still didn't believe that Mauney was responsible. Unfortunately, like Ronald Smith, he didn't do anything to help his case.

The next day, she would either have to charge him or release him. The lab had promised her a report on the blood they found on the hatchet. The circumstantial evidence was overwhelming, but they had failed to make a case on hard facts.

Faye Howard wasn't there when Sharyn arrived home. She sneaked into the house and changed quickly, hoping to avoid a confrontation with her. Things hadn't been pleasant before; after her announcement, they were bound to erupt into war.

She left the house and drove to the Alberts' home that sat squarely on the shore of Diamond Lake. It was a heavy stone structure with leaded glass windows. When she had been a child, they had come to many parties at that house. She had learned to swim in the lake off the pier there. And she had kissed her first boy there late one summer night when she was sixteen.

"Hello Sharyn!" Brenda Albert greeted her at the front door. "I'm so glad you could come tonight."

"Thanks. How's Richard doing?" Sharyn asked, handing her coat to the other woman.

"He's doing so well, Sharyn. You won't believe it!" Brenda whispered. "You know how he was. It's so wonderful to have him home again."

They both looked up at the top of the huge round stairway. The heavy oak rail gleamed in the light from the chandelier. George stood at the top of the stairs. Beside him stood someone Sharyn had never expected to see again.

"Oh, no!" George complained when he saw her. "We were going to surprise you."

"This *is* a surprise," Sharyn assured him.

Richard Albert stood at his father's side. He'd grown into a tall, thick-chested, broad-shouldered man.

"Richard," his mother prompted. "What do you say to Sharyn?"

He stared down at her, his dark eyes not quite acknowledging her.

"Richard," George added.

"Hello," he finally responded.

"Hi, Richard," Sharyn replied. "It's been a long time."

It had been Sharyn's understanding that the Alberts had decided to institutionalize Richard. Now she knew why. With his size and strength, he must have wreaked havoc in their house. He looked like a big puppy let loose on the world. Even worse, she'd heard he had begun to attack his mother. There was a rumor that they had found a home for him when he had picked up his father and laid him on the dining room table. Now Sharyn believed the rumor could have been true.

"He's so much better now," Brenda told her as though she could read her mind. "There are new drugs and therapies. Richard can take advantage of those here. He's like a changed boy."

Boy was hardly the word Sharyn would have used

for the tall, muscular man who came down the stairs at his father's side. When he took her hand in his, it was nearly swallowed by the size. Then he began to squeeze.

Sharyn looked up into his eyes and felt genuine fear. He didn't seem to be seeing her at all. And the grip on her hand continued to grow stronger and more painful.

"That's enough," George reprimanded his only child when he saw Sharyn wince.

"He doesn't know his own strength."

"That's okay," she replied.

They sat down to dinner with a less than jovial mood in the air. Sharyn felt Richard staring at her, and her skin crawled. Why had they brought him back?

"We've moved Richard right back into his old room," Brenda was telling her. "You remember, Sharyn? Over the garage?"

"Of course. How is it, Richard?" she asked him.

"Come and see," he said, getting up from the table abruptly.

"Later," George told him, but Richard had already grabbed Sharyn's hand.

"I guess we're going," she said, following him at the risk of losing her hand.

"He's so particular about things," Brenda said as she followed along. "Everything has got to be a certain way, in a certain place."

Richard led them all up to his room. Sharyn lost feeling in her fingers where his hand closed around them. She recalled being in his room when they were much younger. The one and only time. He had picked her up and tried to toss her out of the window. Even though he had been smaller, he'd had the strength of a bear.

His room was set up for a much younger person. They had left it alone while he'd been gone. Sharyn tried to remember how old he was. Older than her, she was sure, but she wasn't sure how much older. When had they sent him away? How long had it been?

"It's a very nice room," she told him when he finally released her hand. There were sports trophies everywhere. He'd excelled in sports before he'd had to give them up. There were pictures he'd drawn when he was a child and a portrait painted of him when he was a baby.

George and Brenda had poured everything into their child, but nothing could make him the son they wanted. Her mother had told her that it was oxygen deprivation when he was being born. Whatever it was, he would never be the man his parents had hoped would inherit their money and their property. He would probably never be able to live without supervision.

"It's all here," he told her. "Everything."

"He's an avid collector," George explained with a nervous smile.

"Let's go back down to dinner now, Richard," his mother suggested.

George coaxed and pleaded until Richard began to walk with him. Brenda applauded his efforts and asked Sharyn to turn off the light.

Sharyn looked at his collection of trinkets on his dresser. Bottle caps in a neat row. A charm bracelet and some green rocks. There were shells and a piece of green ribbon, a ring with a piece of blue glass in it and a heart-shaped pin with a pearl in it. She switched off the light and shook her head.

They had barely finished dinner when Richard insisted on cleaning off the table. Brenda smiled, and George preened at his son's helpfulness. Under it all was a tension that threatened to break at any moment. They'd thought he would be better. They'd thought drugs or therapy could control him, make him more human. More normal. But he would never lead a normal life, not in the sense they wanted for him.

When Brenda had taken him up for his medication, Sharyn tackled George about seeing Richard out on the lake.

"It had to be someone else," he told her bluntly.

"I know what I saw, George. It was Richard."

He looked at his hands. "He is better now. More lucid. He was tired tonight."

Sharyn put her hand on his shoulder. "He shouldn't be out without supervision."

"I know. Thanks, Sharyn. We'll watch him more closely. It won't happen again."

Sharyn said good night to them and drove home, thinking that there were worse things than death.

Chapter Nine

The deputies had torn apart both the school and Mauney's house but couldn't find a pair of the gray cotton work gloves. Nick had put some of the small fibers into a plastic bag to help them with identification. After emptying out the dumpster and sifting through everything in the old toolshed, they didn't find so much as a thread.

That coupled with the lab report verifying that it was squirrel blood on the hatchet led Sharyn into the uncomfortable position of having to release George Mauney.

The DA was furious. "This is incompetence," he blustered. "You can't find evidence to convict a killer?"

Sharyn let him rant, then calmly looked across her desk at him. "We found nothing substantial that could lead us to believe that George Mauney is the killer."

"He was there," he argued.

"So were a lot of other people who can't account for their exact whereabouts that night. People were still leaving the school and didn't notice that she couldn't get her car started."

"We know he tempered with the girl's car!"

"That's hearsay at best. The students also claim to see Leila Bentley's ghost on the grounds. Even if he did, that's a misdemeanor, and you know it. It's not murder. The best we can do is fine him, and the school will probably fire him."

The DA paced and fumed. "We are not going to look good in all of this, Sheriff. Maybe you don't care about reelection, but I have a career I'm trying to build."

"Build it on someone besides David Mauney," she advised. "We'll find the real killer."

Not filing charges against David Mauney was telling the state that they could proceed with the execution of Ronald Smith. Sharyn felt like her back was against the wall. She didn't want to see an innocent man go to his death, but she couldn't indict another innocent man either. She needed a break in the case, but she wasn't sure where to look. With the loss of David Mauney as a suspect, they were back to grasping at straws. Gray fibers from gloves that could have come from a hundred different sources were not a lot to go on.

She took Ernie with her to the hospital where David Mauney was being held under observation. Susan Mauney was there. Her anxious, tear-stained face told its own story of grief and loss.

"He's going to be released," Sharyn told her. "At least as far as we're concerned."

"What about the hospital?" she asked.

"I've spoken with the head of the department here," Ernie told her. "They plan to release him, with medication, in twenty-four hours. He can come back for therapy."

"It would probably be a good thing if you could leave town for a while," Sharyn told her honestly. "People wanted him to be guilty, so they wouldn't have to be afraid. They aren't going to want to give up so easily. I can keep a deputy with you for a few days, but it might be best if you could leave for a while."

"What about David's job at the school?" his wife asked.

Sharyn glanced at Ernie. "That will have to be handled by the school, ma'am. But it's unlikely that they'll keep him on since he's been accused of tampering with the cars."

Susan nodded. "I understand. I have a sister in Charlotte. We could stay with her for a while. Until things calm down."

"I'm sorry it has to be this way," Sharyn said truthfully.

"You saved his life, Sheriff," she replied. "Don't feel bad for that. Thank you for all your help."

"So why don't I feel like a hero?" Sharyn asked Ernie as they stepped out of the hospital into the sunshine.

"I don't know," he answered. "We did keep him from going to prison."

Sandy Huffman let out a squeal as she saw Sharyn walk out of the hospital parking lot. "Sharyn!" She ran and hugged the sheriff tightly.

"I can go on without you," Ernie offered, watching the woman bear hug the sheriff and trying not to laugh.

"No, that's all right," Sharyn said quickly.

"Yes, let's have that drink, Sharyn," Sandy insisted. "Just look at you! The sheriff of Diamond Springs! Who would have thought, as much as you hated your father doing the job!"

"I'll see you back at the office," Ernie told her. "I think I can handle it alone for a while."

Sharyn smiled wanly and allowed herself to be dragged to Sandy's big pink Cadillac. "I sell Mary Kay cosmetics, as if you didn't notice. I won this baby!"

"That's great," Sharyn said as she climbed into the plush front seat of the car. She watched Ernie drive away in the patrol car with longing in her eyes. She would have never recognized Sandy. She had been plain as a teenager, like Sharyn, but either Mary Kay or time had done her a good turn. She was beautiful and radiant.

Sandy drove them to the only coffee shop in Diamond Springs. They parked the car and walked in the sunshine, then ordered cappuccinos as they entered the shop.

"You look so great," Sandy told her. "I love your hair like that. I remember you used to wear it long, and it was so heavy around your face. This is so light and natural. Did I tell you I was a beautician for a while?"

Sharyn saw Nick sitting at another table and looked away quickly, hoping he wouldn't notice that she was there. All she needed was for Nick to hear all about their escapades as teenagers. Sandy was launching into them loud enough for the whole town to hear.

When their coffee was ready, though, there was no escaping his notice. "Sheriff." He nodded. She nodded her head in return. Nothing more.

"Who was that?" Sandy asked in a loud whisper as they sat back down with their coffee. "He's great."

"He's the coroner," Sharyn whispered.

"You mean he looks at dead people?"

Sharyn nodded. "Professionally."

Sandy looked back at him and waved and smiled. "Well, he could look at my dead body anytime."

It only took a few more waves and smiles before Nick got up to join them. From the pained expression on his face and the stack of papers under his arm, Sharyn guessed that the interruption was less than welcome.

She glanced out the wide window and saw Richard Albert looking back at her. He had his face pressed against the glass. There was no sign of George or Brenda anywhere on the street. She started to get up, looked again, and he was gone.

"Something wrong, Sheriff?" Nick asked.

"No, nothing," she answered, resuming her place at the table. From what she had seen of Richard, she couldn't believe that George and Brenda were allowing him out on his own. He must have wandered away.

Sandy was delighted. She primped and flirted with Nick as though she weren't married.

"We went to school together, you know," she told him with a glance and a wink at Sharyn.

"Really?"

"I'm only in town for the reunion, visiting old friends, that sort of thing."

"Didn't you say you were bringing your husband and your son?" Sharyn asked pointedly.

"Don't be silly!" Sandy slapped her hand playfully. "What fun would that be?" She scooted a little closer to Nick's chair.

Sharyn couldn't recall her old friend being this way. Sandy had been misunderstood and angry as a teenager. Flirting was one of those things she abhorred about pretty girls. They had talked for hours about doing something meaningful with their lives, like joining the Peace Corps. Of course, Sharyn had hated the fact that her father was the sheriff. She would have never believed that she would someday do the job, even if it had seemed feasible that there could be a woman sheriff.

"So." Sandy glanced at both of them. "Are the two of you—"

"No!" It was unanimously echoed by both of them.

"Good. Nicky, did I tell you about the time Sharyn built up her courage and went swimming in the lake?"

Nick smiled at Sharyn as she felt her stomach plunge down to her feet. "No, I don't think I've heard that one."

It was a grueling half hour before Sharyn finally couldn't stand one more embarrassing story about herself. "I have to get back to the office," she told Sandy.

"But you're coming to the dance, right?" Sandy demanded. "And you don't have to wear, like, a dress version of this, do you?" she asked, looking at the brown uniform. "You're not, like, in the military or anything?"

Sharyn had been so sure that it couldn't be any worse. She had been so wrong. She made up her mind at that moment that she wasn't going to the dance, no matter what. Even if her mother and her aunt never spoke to her again. She wasn't going.

"No," Sharyn assured her with a bright smile. "I don't have to wear the uniform."

"Good," Sandy confided, even though Nick was standing beside them in the doorway of the coffee shop. "Between us, it doesn't do a thing for you. Does it, Nicky? Do you need a ride somewhere?"

"No, I'm fine," Sharyn assured her, then accepted her smothering hug. If she never smelled Chanel again either, that would be fine.

Sandy waved, then burned rubber with the back wheels of her pink Cadillac as she peeled out of the parking space.

"Where are the traffic cops when you need them?" Nick asked.

"Is it illegal to spin your tires in the city?" Sharyn remarked.

He nodded. "I have a feeling *she* would be illegal in the city limits."

Sharyn laughed. "You may be right." She caught another glimpse of Richard from the corner of her eye. He was standing at the corner of an alley, staring at her. "I have to go," she told Nick suddenly before she ran to the spot to find it empty.

She looked down the alley, but there was no one there.

"What is it?" Nick asked. He had run after her and stood looking down the alley with her.

"I'm not sure," she answered vaguely. "Maybe I'm just hallucinating."

Suddenly short of words, she ran her hand through her curls, remembering that she had left her hat in the patrol car. "I'll see you later."

She started to walk away, then Nick hailed her. "Are you headed back to the station or was that a lie to sneak away?"

"No, I'm going back. I have some loose ends to tie up before I head over for Carrie's funeral."

"I'll walk with you," he offered, falling into step beside her on the sidewalk.

It was only about a block to the station. The sun was warm, and the air still held a chill, but it was a good time for a walk. Along the sidewalk, dark green bushes were heavily laden with bright red berries. The grand dames of the town, gingerbread houses that had been built there before the civil war, lined the street between the downtown area and the courthouse and sheriff's office.

"So, you released Mauney?" he wondered.

"Everything he said checked out. It was squirrel

blood on the hatchet," she told him. "We couldn't find traces of the glove material anywhere."

Nick nodded. "Better keep looking. There's a killer out there somewhere."

She looked at the children playing in the city park. "I know."

"Are you going to the funeral?"

"Yes. Are you?"

"No." He shook his head. "I didn't know the girl. There's going to be enough press and strangers there for her family to cope with."

She looked at him quickly, then looked away. "That's very . . . thoughtful of you."

He grimaced. "Implying that I can't be thoughtful or considerate?"

"Implying that I didn't think it was part of your nature."

He stopped walking and looked at her. They were almost on the same eye level. "You know, it's good that I'm leaving. You and I haven't been on the same wavelength since the day you started. I don't think we ever will be."

He walked away from her, opened the station door and walked inside without another word. Sharyn was left staring after him without a clue.

The press were still camped out on the front lawn, but they were keeping a lower profile. They sat in their vans and waved as she passed by.

Inside the office, Ed was writing up a report on

a man he'd arrested for breaking and entering. Ernie and Joe were in the interrogation room with Nick, who glowered at her as she entered the room and shut the door.

"What've we got?" she asked, careful not to look directly at Nick.

Nick stood up. "I'm going to check out another lead."

Ernie and Joe looked at Sharyn, who didn't say anything. They sat back in their chairs and looked at their files. Nick and Sharyn were feuding again.

Sharyn looked up as Nick was leaving the room. He closed the door behind him as she was wishing him good luck with his investigation. She sighed. She hated losing Nick's insight, even if they couldn't seem to get along for more than half a case.

"What about Leila's boyfriend?" she turned back to Joe.

"Ed says he had an alibi for Leila's murder; he was with a group of his friends partying all night. This time around, he was working at the aluminum plant. Says his shift supervisor can vouch for him."

"Where does that leave us?" she asked, more of herself than them. "What are we missing?"

"What about the aspect of the car not starting?" Ernie suggested.

"What about it?" Joe questioned.

"I don't know," Ernie answered. "I'm grabbing at straws here."

Sharyn took out the picture that Anita Bentley had given her. She picked up the files on Leila's murder and glanced through them as the two men were bickering back and forth.

There was something wrong. Something that she had sensed immediately when she looked at the photo. Until she picked up the folder full of material, she didn't know what it was.

"Where's her bracelet?" she asked suddenly.

Both men stopped arguing and looked at her.

She looked up at them, holding out the picture. "Her bracelet. This little charm bracelet here." She outlined the area on Leila's wrist. "There's no mention of it in her personal effects."

"It could have fallen out or gotten lost," Joe said with a wave of his hand. "Who knows?"

"Or the killer collects things! Ernie, find me that picture of Carrie Sommers that her mother gave us. The one from before the prom."

Ernie scrambled while Joe sat mystified. Sharyn went for the list of Carrie's personal effects. They studied the picture and the list but couldn't see any difference.

"Look there." Sharyn pointed to the left side of the girl's dress. "Before the corsage was pinned in place. What's that?"

Joe squinted. "I don't see anything."

"It might just be the light reflecting," Ernie said with a shrug.

Sharyn grabbed the phone and called Carrie's mother. Carrie had been wearing a pin on her left shoulder that was covered by the corsage. She didn't want to take the time to remove it since they were running late. It was a small, heart-shaped pin with a pearl at one side. It had belonged to her grandmother.

"So, she was wearing a pin." Joe shook his head.

"Where is it?" Sharyn asked. "It wasn't on her dress. It's not in her personal effects."

"Maybe she took it off."

"Or maybe our murderer is the same man, and he collected both items from his victims."

Even as the words came out of her mouth, Sharyn knew where she had seen the distinctive heart-shaped pin. Her throat felt as though it were being squeezed in a vice. She put down the file she held and closed her eyes.

"Oh no!" She tried to breathe but couldn't find the air to draw into her lungs.

Quickly, she dialed George and Brenda's phone number. There was no answer. She got up and started for the door. "Ernie, you're with me. Joe, call Ed and David in right away. The killer is Richard Albert. He's tall, dark hair, about thirty. He's wearing a green jacket and blue jeans."

"Councilman Albert's son?" Joe asked in disbelief.

She nodded. "I'm going to check out his home.

Arm yourselves. This guy is big, and he's not responsible for his actions. Let's pray he hasn't done anything else."

The front door to the Alberts' home was closed but not locked. There were people doing lawn work in the big yard, but none of them had seen anyone come in or out.

Sharyn didn't waste any time. She drew her grandfather's service revolver and went carefully into the house.

Everything was in place. There wasn't a sound from anywhere. She waved Ernie to the top of the house while she checked out the ground floor. Carefully, moving from room to room, she made it into the kitchen. Brenda Albert was lying on the kitchen table, very still, with a pair of pantyhose wrapped around her neck.

Sharyn's heart skipped a beat as she checked around the room and the pantry but saw no sign of Richard. "Brenda?" she whispered, hoping the woman was all right.

"Sharyn," the other woman whimpered softly. "Sharyn!"

She went to her and untied the pantyhose from around her neck.

"He wanted to kill me, Sharyn," Brenda sobbed, almost unintelligibly. "He thought he had, but I was very still and didn't move. He spread out my dress around me and kissed my forehead. Then he left."

Brenda cried into Sharyn's shoulder. "Where is he now?" she asked the other woman.

"I think he wanted to go to the Sommers' girl's funeral. I don't know why, Sharyn. I know he didn't kill her. He wouldn't have killed someone. Not when we've just brought him home! It's like *we* killed her, isn't it? We let him loose again. After that other poor girl was killed. George was afraid that he did that, you know. He didn't want to believe it, but that's why he sent him away. The next day. Oh, Sharyn! What have we done?"

Ernie came into the kitchen and held up the charm bracelet and the pin already sealed in plastic. "Right where you said it would be, Sheriff. No sign of the boy, though."

"Get an ambulance here, Ernie," She turned back to Brenda. "Where's George, Brenda?"

"He's gone looking for him, I think. He took his rifle."

"You think they went to the funeral?"

"I think Richard wanted to go to the funeral. He was mad that he couldn't go to the last one for poor Leila Bentley."

Sharyn looked at Ernie. "Stay with her until the medics get here. I'll leave the patrol car for you. Brenda, I'm borrowing the Jeep."

Brenda was beyond hearing as she sobbed into her hands.

"Be careful, Sharyn," Ernie advised grimly.

"Meet you at the church."

Chapter Ten

Sharyn didn't know what would have caused Richard to murder those two girls. It made the question of whether her father had been involved in a cover-up even more complicated. If he had known that George's son killed Leila Bentley, would he have allowed George to send the boy away?

The two men were like brothers. Sharyn felt certain that even her mother wouldn't know the answer to that question.

She drove the Jeep toward the church where the funeral service was already in progress. She felt certain Richard wasn't armed, but she knew how strong he was. She couldn't handle him physically. She didn't want to hurt him, but she knew she would have to commit to any action that would take him off the street. He had to be confined. He would have to be put on trial for the murder of the two girls.

What had made George go out looking for his son? Had he finally realized that he couldn't be free? Richard must have doubled back to the house and caught his mother alone. She couldn't imagine what Dr. Hartsell would make of Richard's problems. She now knew, though, that he had been describing George's son they day they had talked. She just hadn't realized it at the time.

As she had expected, nearly the whole town had turned out at the church. Diamond Springs was a close-knit community. Losing a beautiful, intelligent girl like Carrie Sommers was a loss to them all. And murder was something unusual. People might see crimes on television and read about them in the papers, but they still felt like they were isolated from them.

That was one thing Sharyn and her father had always disagreed on. Sharyn felt that the people of Diamond Springs should realize that the world wasn't the same place where they grew up. Her father felt as if it was his duty to provide a place out of time for them. They had debated the point many times before he died. There was never a mutual agreement on what should be done.

Parking had overrun the lots into the streets and across part of the cemetery park. Music swelled out from the church, shivering through the skeletal branches of the old trees. The sun had gone behind a layer of heavy gray clouds as though it were too ashamed to shine on such a terrible day.

Joe was at the end of the first lot. Sharyn parked the Jeep on a hillside and ran to tell him what had happened, watching for Richard as she went.

"George Albert is stalking his son out here somewhere," she explained. "He's armed."

"Great," Joe grunted. "That's what we need in all this mess."

"Richard's probably not armed, but he's strong as an ox. Don't take chances with him, Joe."

"You got it." He nodded. "Ed's inside the church. David's on the other side of the cemetery. Nick is on his way out."

"What for?" she wondered.

He shrugged. "Backup? He is a duly authorized deputy. I called the highway patrol. They're sending out some people as soon as they can."

She nodded. "I'm going to walk the perimeter. He could be anywhere."

Joe snorted. "At least I'm not a pretty blonde."

She turned to walk away from him.

"Sheriff?" He called her back.

"Yeah?"

"I guess we all owe you an apology. You were right."

"Thanks," she said. "I wish it felt better."

The cemetery itself was almost empty. The grave

was set up, and a few of the people from the funeral home stood around it, setting out flowers and chairs for the graveside service. Gravestones dating back a hundred years stood up to face the coming storm or leaned at odd angles to the ground.

Walking carefully past them all, Sharyn watched for George or his son. Did George mean to try to bring the boy into custody? Or was he planning on trying to help him run again? Even worse, she feared that he knew the truth and wanted to end the problem. The idea of having to take George into custody for killing his son was terrible. It was bad enough to put Richard away forever. George and Brenda were like family.

She waved to David at the other side of the cemetery. He gave her the all clear sign. Joe would have spoken to him on the radio after she explained everything. He would know that he was looking for both men.

Sharyn wondered if Caison Talbot had been protecting George's secret as well. Had he really been serving his own selfish ends? Or had he been part of the cover-up that had saved Richard the first time?

There was a movement to her left. She dropped down to the frozen ground at once, hiding behind a tombstone with a weeping angel on it. Her breath was frosty in the air before her. She held her gun carefully, ready to fire if she needed to, hoping she wouldn't be called on to shoot George or Richard.

A jeans-clad leg came into view around the corner of the tombstone. She didn't take any chances. With a quick movement she'd learned in self-defense class, she brought the man down to the ground. She moved to stand over him quickly, hearing the breath wheeze out of his lungs as he fell. She held her gun steady on him, her foot on his lower back.

"Put your hands behind your head and spread your legs!"

He did as he was told, then spit out some of the dirt he'd tasted when he hit the ground. "I surrender," he told her. "I don't have a white flag, but I promise not to try anything."

"Nick!"

He rolled over and faced her. "I thought I could help. I didn't come to be target practice."

"Where's your duly authorized uniform?"

"My dog ate it?" he proposed.

"Get up," she commanded. "We don't have time for games."

"Games?" he echoed, getting up and following her. "I came out to help."

"Stay out of the way."

"I'm trained. I've been in the field before."

The words "with your father" hung in the air, but

even Nick was wise enough not to speak them aloud.

"Then walk toward the church. They should be finished and moving outside soon. We don't want George taking potshots at his son through a crowd of mourners."

He glanced at her, but she was already walking away from him.

Sharyn fumed. That was all she needed was a rookie in the field. Ed, Joe and David were all highly trained deputies. They knew what they were doing. Nick was a coroner. He belonged in an office. Preferably in New York.

Something hit her hard in the back of the head, and she stumbled, then went down on one knee. She felt rough hands push her down to the ground, and she lay back, winded and in pain. Her head was throbbing, her vision blurred.

In the next instant, he was on her. Richard straddled her body and put his hands against her throat.

"Richard," she rasped. "It's me, Sharyn."

She wanted to say that she wasn't pretty or blond, but the words wouldn't come. She felt sick and dazed. He was slowly squeezing the life out of her.

"Get up!" She heard George say. "Get off of her."

Richard paused and looked back at his father. "I've always wanted to kill her," he said matter-of-factly. "Remember that time I almost threw her out of the window? Go away. Let me do what I need to do."

"Why?" George asked.

Sharyn could tell George was crying. When the pressure against her throat eased away, she started to think again. Her head still felt like something had exploded in it. She realized that she had dropped her gun. She reached out a hand to find it.

"Because she reminds me of something. I don't know what."

"Don't hurt her, Richard," George begged him. "Please."

"Go away. She's not pretty like the other ones. Like Mom."

"What are you saying, Richard?"

"Nothing!" Richard hissed. "Go away and leave me alone."

"Move off of her, son," George told him. "Don't make me hurt you."

Richard ignored him and put his hands around Sharyn's throat again. She used his turn to get her leg into place and kicked him away from her. He snarled at her and half turned to hit her with the hammer he held in his hand.

"Put it down," she said in a husky voice. "Now."

He looked down the barrel of her grandfather's gun, and with an enraged howl, he launched himself at her again.

Sharyn fired once and hit him, point blank, in the chest.

"Put it down, Mr. Albert," David yelled from behind the grieving father.

George fell to the ground beside his dying son and wept.

"Over here!" Sharyn heard David yell to the others. She sat back on the cold ground, her gun in her lap.

"What happened?" Joe demanded.

"Sharyn!" Ernie screamed, falling over the tombstone beside her to reach her side.

Before the medics could arrive, Nick had stepped in and pronounced Richard Albert dead, and Sheriff Sharyn Howard alive and kicking but with a husky new voice.

"Yeah, go away," she said to him in her hoarse croak.

"I'm a doctor, you know," he argued.

"And if I was bleeding to death, I'd consider it."

"You should have an X ray of that stubborn head of yours," he said as she winced when he touched the back of her head.

"I'll do that," she promised.

The mourners in the church had spilled out and were standing outside watching and waiting to see what had happened. The graveside service was forgotten momentarily as they struggled to see George Albert and his son. There was a rumor that the sheriff was dead. It was squashed immediately when the crowd saw her stand and walk to Councilman Albert's side, holstering her gun as she went.

"George."

"You don't have to say anything."

"I'm so sorry."

His face crumpled. "He was all we had. They said that he could be normal with drugs and therapy. We couldn't leave him there forever."

"He attacked Brenda. She's okay."

"How will I ever forgive myself?"

"What did the doctors say, George? What made him this way?"

"He couldn't separate reality from fantasy. It was like a game he was playing with those girls. He didn't exactly mean to harm them."

"He wanted to kill me," she reminded him, moving her stiff neck uncomfortably.

"He hated you. I don't know why. Something he had seen that he didn't understand. I'm so sorry, Sharyn."

She turned away from him. *Did you know that he had killed Leila Bentley before you sent him away? Did my father know?*

"You're sure that you're okay, Sheriff?" Ernie asked. "The medics are here. You could go in for a checkup."

"I'm fine," she told him blankly. "I'm going home for a while."

* * *

Sharyn's younger sister, Kristie, was home from college for a few days. Sharyn and her mother exchanged angry looks across her sister's shoulder. For them it was unspoken language that meant they would be on friendly terms with Kristie there. She hated to see them fight.

"What a case!" Kristie exclaimed as they sat down. "You're going to be famous."

"I think that's infamous, right now," Sharyn remarked, glad to see her sister's happy young face after the sadness at Carrie's funeral.

They had talked for a few minutes about Kristie's experiences at school since Christmas, her grades and her friends. Their mother came in with some sassafras tea and they sat together, drinking it in silence for a few minutes.

"Poor Carrie," Kristie said, swirling the milk into her tea.

"You knew her?" Sharyn wondered.

Kristie had been different in high school from Sharyn. She had been pretty and popular, a cheerleader and a tireless worker. She had missed a scholarship to the college of her choice by a few points. It had been the same year their father had died. Sharyn had picked up the tab for what her mother couldn't afford.

"She was a junior when I was a senior," Kristie

said. "But I met her on the cheerleading squad. We went out together a few times. She was a nice person."

"I heard the Mauneys left town," Faye Howard added. "I'm glad he's gone. The school wasn't safe with him there. I shudder to think the two of you went to school with him there."

Kristie shrugged. "Mr. Mauney always came out and gave me a hand. He helped everyone with their cars when they had trouble."

"He tampered with your car?" Sharyn asked.

"He's a little rough around the edges, but I could tell he really wanted to make contact, you know? He was always standing around watching everyone."

The three women sat quietly in the parlor and drank their tea. Sharyn didn't want to think that Richard could have killed Kristie, but she knew it was true. It could have been any girl at the school.

"What about George and Brenda?" her mother asked with a forced smile.

Sharyn swallowed some of her tea, surprised that her mother spoke to her. "They've closed up the house and are going up north somewhere for a while. The DA decided against charging George since they couldn't prove that he knew Richard had killed Leila."

"What about Daddy?" Kristie asked, looking at her mother and sister. "Did he help send that man to prison to give George time to send Richard away?"

Faye Howard stood up stiffly. "Dinner's going to be ready soon. I'll be in the kitchen."

Kristie watched her mother leave the room, then turned to her sister. "What's with her?"

Sharyn set down her cup. "She's afraid."

"Of what?"

"The truth," Sharyn replied. "Come on. Let's go eat."

"Are you afraid, too?" Kristie wondered.

Sharyn hugged her sister, then looked down into her bright blue eyes. "We'll never know the answer to that question, Kristie. I'm going to think that Dad wouldn't have done anything like that. Even to help an old friend."

The two sisters walked into the kitchen where the smell of brownies made it feel like home.

Epilogue

Sharyn sat at the reunion dance, watching the colored lights flash across the ceiling and drinking awful punch from a paper cup that leaked. She was still a little brusied from her encounter in the cemetery. But everything had fallen into place.

They found several pairs of gray garden gloves in Richard's room, along with some other trophies. The FBI were looking at them as evidence in other murders.

They had determined that Richard had taken a boat across the lake to the high school to commit both murders. The school was visible from his house. They found more gloves, some plastic bags, another hammer with blood and hair on it and part of Carrie's corsage.

There was no doubt that Richard Albert murdered

the two girls. But there were too many unanswered questions for Sharyn to like the end results. Despite Dr. Hartsell's explaining the mental problems Richard exhibited, to her and to an inquest, she was still baffled. What made a child into a demon? Surely a lack of oxygen wasn't the answer.

As for her father and Caison Talbot, they were both cleared of any charges at the inquest, although that was done quickly and quietly. No one wanted to dig any deeper. It was sad and awful enough to watch George Albert lose everything.

Sharyn had visited both the Bentleys and the Sommerses on a Saturday morning when she should have been home having her dress fitted. Both sets of parents were relieved that it was over. Stuart Bentley was skeptical. After all, they had already arrested his daughter's murderer once.

Mike Dakin had been pleased and surprised that it had worked out for Ronnie Smith and for Sharyn. He would be working with Ronnie's lawyer to free him the following week. The state had set up a compensation fund for him. Sharyn couldn't imagine what could start to compensate the man for the loss of ten years of his life.

Which brought Sharyn up against a wall of nothing to do, nowhere to run. She went home and found her Aunt Selma working with Kristie and her mother to finish her dress. Only two hours more of being stuck and praised and reminded to hold her shoulders back before the dress was ready.

When it was done and the magical night was upon her, Kristie worked on her stubborn hair and did her make up. Sharyn had to admit that she didn't look as bad as she thought that she would. Her eyes were bright. Her lipstick was a good shade for her. The hated green satin looked presentable. Before she knew it, she had let them talk her into going to the dance. Kristie had driven her to the school so that she wouldn't change her mind and was coming back for her at midnight after she'd had a wonderful time.

Sharyn sighed and kicked at the hem of her dress. It was as bad as it had been ten years ago, except that Sandy was the belle of the ball this time, and she had no one to make fun of the other girls with. She sat on a chair near the punch table for two hours. Several people she had known in school came up to congratulate her on solving the murder case. Several others came to ask her to sign their programs as the sheriff of Diamond Springs.

It was a disaster. She was getting ready to get up and call a taxi when Ed, Ernie and Joe came in through the door. Her heart raced. This was even better. She would have a good excuse for cutting out early if something had happened that needed her attention.

"Sheriff?" Ed asked in amazement, staring at her from head to toe. "You look great!"

"Yeah," Joe agreed. "I wouldn't have known it was you!"

"Thanks," she replied, feeling dubiously honored. "Is something wrong?"

Ernie smiled and played with his moustache. It was then that she noticed that they were all wearing their dress uniforms.

"Could I have this dance?" Ernie asked.

Sharyn smiled despite herself. "You have to be kidding."

"Not at all." He held out his hand to her. "I think I can dance without embarrassing you."

And that was what they all did. For almost two hours, the three men kept her company, dancing and talking, getting punch and posing for pictures with her. It was midnight before they left, claiming an early day with tons of paperwork.

"My boss is a real stickler," Ed confided. "She gets what she goes after."

Sharyn smiled and felt her cheeks turn red. "I'm sure she's feeling too good about being right to care."

"I hope you're right," he answered. "She did one whale of a job."

Sharyn waved to the three men as they left. She laughed to herself, not able to erase the smile from her face. They had come to rescue her. She wasn't sure if she should feel flattered or insulted.

She decided that she would be flattered. They were good men.

It was the last dance. The lights went down low and the music was soft. It was the song she remembered being played for the sweethearts' dance ten years before. She had left while it was playing.

"Dance?" The question was thrown out absently.

She looked up. "Nick?"

He took her hand and pulled her to her feet. He wrapped his arm around her waist and held her hand firmly in check. "Don't even think about it. You're not wearing your gun."

She relaxed as much as she could in that position. He was wearing a tuxedo, something that very few of the men had done that night. Most had worn suits and a few had come in jeans and sweaters. He looked dark and demonic with his usual evil smile.

"I've decided I'm not quitting," he told her without missing a step.

Sharyn frowned. "Oh, that's too bad. We just hired the new coroner yesterday."

He grinned. "I checked. You had one other applicant, and he was sixty-seven years old."

"Why?" she wondered as he swung her into a turn.

He considered her question. "Let's just say that I

might have found a way to work with my personal problem."

"Oh?"

He dipped her low over his arm, and she squeaked, holding on to his shoulder tightly. He chuckled darkly. "Patience is a virtue, Sharyn. One I'm learning to cultivate."

Sharyn sighed. "I was hoping that you really were leaving this time."

"Really?" he asked sharply, his grip a little tighter on her hand.

She laughed, wondering if her freckles and red hair looked as pretty as they felt. "No, not really," she admitted. Then when he looked relieved, an imp pushed her to add, "A good coroner is hard to find."

He sighed heavily. "Patience," he whispered. "Patience."

"Good luck," she whispered back.